Following Frankie

Book Four in the Boone Series

by Jim Hartsell

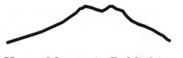

House Mountain Publishing

This is a work of fiction. Any resemblance to persons living or dead is coincidental.

Cover design by:
www.nickcastledesign.com

ISBN 978-1-7346738-5-2

Also by Jim Hartsell

The Boone Series:

Pushing Back   Book One
Matching Scars   Book Two
Keeping Secrets   Book Three

Other Fiction:

Tango
Rock, Paper, Scissors
Journey

Children's Books:

Father and Sister Radish and the Rose-
    Colored Glasses
The Box of Toys
The Boy and His Mountain
The Noise in the Woods
(All children's titles also available in Spanish)

Non-Fiction:

Glimpses
Sisyphus and the Itsy-Bitsy Spider (out of print)

Chapter One

"Which way, Frankie?"

I look over at her and she looks back at me. We're at a T intersection, about two miles from the home, and as far as I'm concerned it doesn't matter whether we turn left or right. There's a car coming up behind us, so I ask her again.

"Which way? C'mon, girl, we got to get moving."

She turns her head to the right and keeps it there, so I turn right. Now I'm driving into the sun and I can't hardly see, but pretty soon we're under some trees and it's a lot better.

I'm not sure, but I think if we had turned left we would have gone right by that old run-down house where I took Frankie to run that time, and I try to remember what Nancy said was out past it. I know she told me, but I can't remember, so I give up and try to concentrate on the road. I don't like thinking about Nancy right now, but I can't get her out of my head.

"You think she would've come with us, girl?"

Frankie's got her nose up against the top of the window, where I've got it down just a crack. She doesn't even look around.

"Well, I think she probably would have if I could have gotten anywhere near her, but I bet Stan is on her all the time," I say to Frankie. "She . . . ." I can't think of anything else to say, so I look out ahead. There's another intersection coming up, and I pull up right behind a big GMC. It says Denali on the back, and I bet it's half again as big as my truck.

"Damn, Frankie, look at that thing." It's black and looks like it's never had a speck of dust on it.

When the light changes it goes straight through and I follow, since I'm not really going anywhere in particular. The road curves back and forth and sometimes the sun's straight ahead, but mostly not, and after a while the road kind of straightens out and the sun is coming in my window.

We go about thirty or forty miles and the Denali puts on its turn signal. I look up ahead and all I can see is a gravel road that's probably a driveway. The GMC turns in there and we go on past.

We must be driving right along the Smokies. They're on my left and seems like they go on forever. I never knew they were so big. Knoxville is behind us; I made it around the edge of it, not sure exactly how, but I didn't have to go through all that mess that

Nancy drove us into that time we went to Market Square. Wonder when Stan will let her go back down there again. Probably not for a long time.

Wonder who she'll take with her then.

Frankie is getting restless and I realize that she's been in this truck for a while now. I start looking for a place to pull over where I can get her out on the leash and walk her around some.

It takes about another fifteen minutes, but there's a convenience store that has a picnic table back in the trees behind it and I pull in and park over on the side.

Frankie can't wait to get out of the truck and she almost pulls the leash out of my hand, but in a second we're back under the trees and she's moving back and forth, nose to the ground, looking for a place to squat.

She finally makes up her mind and I'm standing there just looking around when I hear a door slam and look over at the back of the store. There's a guy standing there with his arms crossed looking at me like he just caught me trying to break into a car or something.

"What the hell do you think you're doing?" he shouts at me.

"Nothing," I say.

"You think my yard's your dog's toilet?"

I look around some more and I can barely see a

doublewide at the back of the trees, with a bunch of bushes growing up around it. It sure didn't look like anybody's yard when I pulled in, but I guess it's his.

"Sorry, man, I didn't know you lived here."

He takes a step toward me.

"Listen, I just didn't see your place back there. I'll get Frankie back in the truck and we'll get out of your way."

"There better not be any dog shit in my yard, you hear me?"

"There's not, man, she just had to pee. C'mon, Frankie, let's get out of here."

He takes another step and I'm thinking, he doesn't have to be an asshole about this, but it's sure starting to look like that's what's happening. I figure I'd better get on out of here before I end up saying something. Frankie sees how this guy is acting and she growls a little, real low.

"You'd best not sic that dog on me, boy!" He's shouting again, and I'm pulling Frankie toward the truck and lifting her up into the seat.

When I look around after I close the door he's stopped and he's just standing there waiting. I go around to the driver's side and get in, start the truck, and back out into the parking lot.

He's standing at the edge of the lot, pointing over to his left, and he says, "This is private property. Can't you read?"

4

I look where he's waving his arm and all I see are trees.

"Read what?" I don't know whether or not he can hear me, so I kind of shrug and raise up my hands.

"That sign right there," he says, still real mad, and he looks over and stops waving his arm for a second. Then he goes over to one of the trees and bends down and picks up a sign off the ground. He stands there holding it in both hands staring down at it, shaking his head.

He's brushing the dirt off of it when we pull back out on the road. We go about forty more miles or so and stop at a grocery store that has a big parking lot. When I take Frankie out on her leash nobody even notices me, and the place is open all night. I find a place over on the edge of the lot, away from everybody else, and tell Frankie to stay in the truck. I go into the store to get some food for us and I'm thinking I might just spend the night here. It's as good a place as any, and I don't see any signs that say I can't.

When I come out of the grocery store there's somebody standing beside the truck, looking through the window at Frankie. When I'm about twenty feet away this guy raises his hand up over his head, and he's got some kind of hammer. It looks like that bastard's about to steal my dog, so I drop the bags and take off running.

"Hey! Wait just a damn minute!"

The guy drops his hand down and turns to face me. Turns out it's not a guy, it's a girl. She looks up at me like she's about ready to swing on me.

"Don't you know any better than to leave an animal trapped inside a car like that? You know how hot it can get inside behind all that glass? Are you trying to kill this poor dog?"

She pushes her hair back out of her face and stares at me.

"Well?"

"Well, what?"

"Well, get him out of there before he dies of heat stroke! Never mind, I'll do it myself." She raises up the hammer again and turns back toward the window.

I jump in between her and my truck and she acts like she's going to swing anyway, and then drops the hammer and takes a step back. "So get him out of that truck. I'll bet he's dying for a drink of water."

"Frankie's not a he, and I was only gone a couple of minutes."

"Okay, so get her out." She's still mad as hell, and I don't get it. It's not that hot today, and most of the truck is under a shade tree.

I reach in and put Frankie's leash on and she jumps down out of the truck. I got to admit it's a little hot in there, but not bad and she looks fine to me.

"See? She's fine."

The girl is a couple of steps back from where she was, and hunkered down so she and Frankie are eye to eye. She just squats there, waiting, and Frankie takes a step toward her. She puts out her hand and Frankie sniffs the back of it and then licks it.

I'm watching all this and thinking, Frankie has to know how mad she was, swinging that hammer around and all that, yelling at me like I'm some kind of stupid kid. Any other time she'd be growling. Now she's more curious than anything else.

"What a good girl, Frankie, you're a beauty, aren't you? Look how good you are," the girl is talking real soft and scratching Frankie behind the ear and Frankie looks like she's in heaven. I'm standing there holding the leash and looking around and finally I say, "Weren't you all about her getting a drink? Like she was dying of thirst or something?"

The girl looks up at me and just like that she's mad again and says, "That's right. You had her locked up, didn't you?" She stares at me for a second and then back at Frankie. "Didn't he, you big, beautiful girl, you," and she's back to not mad at all.

"You know you can't just go around busting out people's windows," I say, and she stands up again and wipes her hands on her jeans. "I mean, you'd get your ass thrown in jail."

"Shows how much you know," she says. "Until you

7

get another hour down this road you're still in Tennessee, and we have a Good Samaritan law. You never heard of that, did you?"

She looks away and it's like I've been cut loose, like I was pinned against the truck before. She's got the strongest stare I've ever seen except for Daddy, and his was just mean. Hers isn't like that at all, but it sure is powerful.

I lead Frankie around to the back where her dishes are and raise the hatch and drop the tailgate. She looks inside while I crawl in to get the dish and the gallon jug of water I keep with it.

"Is that where you live?"

At first I don't answer, because I figure she's making fun of me, but when I get Frankie's water down in front of her I say, "For right now, yeah."

"That is great," she says. "You're never away from home."

I look up at her and she's smiling, and it takes me a second to realize that she's not making fun of me or looking down on me.

A horn blows from over close to the store and she says, "Gotta go. You take good care of Frankie, okay?" She looks around and then picks up the hammer where she had dropped it. "My boss will kill me if I lose any of his precious tools." She takes off across the parking lot and climbs into a van that has "Ocoee!" painted on the side.

The van backs out of the space and heads toward the highway and then turns. It's heading toward me and then swings around so the passenger window is closest. She has the window down and says, "What's your name?"

"Boone."

"Abigail." And then she's gone, almost before I can get my hand up to wave goodbye.

I look down at Frankie. "What did you think about that, girl?"

Frankie doesn't answer, but I know what I think. I think I just got my ass kicked by a girl with maybe the best smile I've ever seen.

The next morning the traffic on the highway starts around six and keeps getting louder and louder. I've never been in a place where I couldn't just wake up whenever I wanted to, at least since Daddy's been gone.

He used to make enough noise in the morning so that everybody was awake by the time he took off. If he had work sometimes that was pretty early, a lot earlier than any of the rest of us had to get up, but either he didn't care that he woke us all up or he just did it out of meanness.

Anyway, for the last couple of years I've gone to bed whenever I want to and gotten up the same way. I've never lived this close to this much traffic, and I already know I don't like it. It makes me wish I was back up in Gamaliel's old place.

"Tonight we'll find a place to park that's away from all this noise," I tell Frankie. "This is an awful way to have to wake up."

She doesn't answer me, but I think that's because she wants me to take her outside. I grab the leash and open up the back of the truck.

When I lived at home or Gamaliel's place, I could open the door and let Frankie go look for a place to pee while I followed along in a few minutes. At the old folks home she had to be on a leash, but we were still only a few steps from the yard. Here we're standing in a parking lot and even though we parked under a tree, there's nothing but gravel and pavement all around us.

"Come on, Frankie," I say. "Never lived in a place where I had to go looking for grass."

We finally find a place next to a drainage ditch that's dirt instead of gravel and has a few sprigs of grass. It's pitiful, but Frankie's about to bust by now and she doesn't care. I hold her leash and think about what Melvin told me, about carrying around little plastic bags so I could pick up dog shit. I guess he was serious.

When we start back up toward the truck Frankie is nosing around, just checking out the area, and all of a sudden her head goes up and her tail starts wagging. Then she's pulling me up the hill and across

10

the gravel back to the tree, and I look up to see Abigail waving at us.

Chapter Two

She holds up a paper bag. "I brought breakfast."

Then she hops off the tailgate and squats down in front of Frankie, who goes to her like she's known Abigail all her life.

"Hello, Frankie, how did you sleep? Did you have a good nap?"

I'm standing there wondering about what is in that bag. Smells like bacon, and I realize how hungry I am. Abigail looks up at me and I don't even notice, since I'm staring at the bag on the tailgate. She laughs and I jerk a little and look down at her. I can feel my face getting red.

"Go ahead," she says. "There's a couple of biscuits in there with eggs and Benton's bacon and two cups of coffee. No coffee for you, you beautiful girl," and she's back to Frankie and I might as well not be standing there.

I tie Frankie's leash to the back bumper and get out her food and water dishes. After I fill them up I say, "Whenever you're ready, girl, here's breakfast."

Frankie barely looks back at me but Abigail grins at me. "Get the bag, Boone. Time for our breakfast too. You ever had Benton's bacon before?"

I shake my head.

"Well, you're in for a treat. Some people say it's better than sex, but I can't go that far," and she winks at me.

She unwraps her biscuit and takes a big bite, chews for a minute and then washes it down with a sip of coffee. She looks over at me and starts laughing again. "You going to try that? If you don't get going Frankie's going to steal it right out of your hand!"

I look down and Frankie's about six inches away from my food and her nose is quivering. When I hold it up over my head she looks at me like I'm the bad guy and goes back to her dish. I take a bite.

"Well?"

I haven't finished chewing but I'm about ready to take another bite. I can't believe how good this bacon is. Instead of another bite I finish the one I'm working on and say, "Damn. That's good stuff."

"Told you. The coffee's okay, but what Mr. Benton really knows how to do is cure meat."

I nod.

"He's just down the road here, you know."

I nod again, thinking about getting a sip of the okay coffee and also about sex with Abigail. I've

14

never done it with anybody and I figure there's a thousand different ways to mess it up, but I'd sure like to see what it's like. She looks really good sitting there, and strong, like she lifts weights or something. I figure if I try anything and she's not interested I'd be flat on my back in about ten seconds.

Frankie comes nosing around and when I look down I see her food bowl still has a little food in it. "Finish that up, girl, while I eat this, and if you're still hungry we'll get you some more."

Abigail stands up and stretches, reaching her arms up to the sky. She's a little shorter than I am. She bends over and puts her palms flat on the pavement and then straightens up. She looks over at me. "You know you're staring, right?"

"Sorry," I say. I'm confused and embarrassed that I got caught, but what I mainly want to do is keep on staring. That's probably the wrong thing to do, so I check Frankie's food dish and see that it's almost empty. I pour the last few bits back into the bag.

She sits back down and picks up her coffee cup. After taking another sip and her next-to-last bite of biscuit, she says, "Now what?"

I'm not sure what she's talking about. Is this about me staring at her? I don't say anything.

She waits a second and then says, "So now what? Are you going south from here? Staying under this tree for a while? Going back to wherever you came from?"

"I don't know."

"Really?"

I nod. "Really. This friend of mine told me I should go on a road trip, and, well, there wasn't much reason to stick around anyway, so I thought why the hell not? Just go, you know, and see what happens."

"So what did your parents say about that?"

I don't answer, and I'm starting to feel kind of uncomfortable talking about this. I look down and Frankie is just sitting there looking at me like she's listening, like she wants to know too.

For a long time I'm quiet, thinking about Mark, and Tiny, and Nancy, and Jerry, and Gamaliel, and Momma and Daddy and Frankie and Hannah, but mostly about Gamaliel and how much I miss him.

That old man was rough as a cob, but I sure loved him, and we were getting along great. If the stupid son of a bitch hadn't gone and died on me things would still be great. I know that, like I know there's a lot he still hadn't taught me.

He would have known what to do about Jerry, and Momma's new boyfriend Jake, and me screwing things up with Nancy over and over again. I miss him like crazy and if I keep on thinking like this I'm going to start crying in front of Abigail and she'll think I'm just some little kid running away from home and probably start laughing at me.

I finally look over at Abigail. "They didn't say anything."

"Why not?"

I slide off the tailgate and untie Frankie. "Ready to get going?" She pulls at her leash and I say, "Okay, one more bathroom break and then we'll go."

Abigail is still sitting on the tailgate and I turn to her. "Thanks for the biscuit. How much do I owe you?"

She shakes her head. "Go take care of your dog."

She's gone when we get back to the truck. There's a torn piece of paper under the windshield wiper and I pull it out.

It's from Abigail. "My bad," it says. "I got nosy. Give me a call if you come back through here. Maybe you can buy me a biscuit." There's a number underneath her name, and I put the paper in the cupholder in the door.

We get loaded up and head out in the same direction we were going, away from home. It still feels like home, even though I got no family there anymore and no place to live.

Wonder how long it will take for me to stop thinking that's where home is.

We come to an intersection and there are signs about Ocoee River Rafting and I remember that was the word painted on Abigail's van. I pull over into the turn lane and we go left, toward the mountains.

"Not sure why I'm doing this, Frankie," I say. "We probably won't see her. It's not like she's going to be standing on the side of the road waiting for us to come driving by."

By the middle of the day we are past the Ocoee River and the Ocoee Lake and through some place called Ducktown and heading into North Carolina and, sure enough, Abigail was not out on the side of the road anywhere waiting for us to come by.

We spend the night in Franklin and keep heading east the next day. Pretty soon I can tell we're leaving the mountains; I can see farther every direction I look.

Since we don't really know where we're going, I let Frankie pick every other time we come to a red light. I use my turns to get us back headed east if we're going in some other direction, but neither one of us is worrying about it too much.

Frankie's nose is glued to the top of the window where I've left it open a crack for her. I'll bet there's a thousand new smells out there. I reach over and scratch behind her ears and put my hand back on the wheel. There are signs that say Charlotte is coming up soon, and I don't remember Melvin talking about anyplace like that. The next gas station we come to I pull in, fill up the truck, and pull away from the pumps over to the edge of the lot. Maybe it's time to take a look at Melvin's map. Not because I care that much about where we're going, but I am a little curious about what's up ahead of us.

What I see coming up is Charlotte. It looks big on the map, so I unfold it until I can see Knoxville. Charlotte is definitely bigger than Knoxville, so there's no way I'm going there. There has to be some way around it. The map shows the Atlantic Ocean not too far away, and I'd sure like to see that while I'm this close. I'm already kind of south of Charlotte, so that seems like the best way around it. I might have to ignore Frankie's suggestions about which way to turn for the next little while.

I'm picking my way along, heading more or less toward the sun. It's still morning, so I figure that'll keep us headed in the right direction if I want to see the ocean. It's hard for me to imagine not seeing anything but water when I look out, but that's what it's supposed to be like. Water as far as you can see. I've always had the mountains to kind of rest my eyes against, and I don't know if I'll like not having something to hang on to.

Frankie's not bothered by me ignoring her directions. As usual, she's got her nose glued to that little space where I have the window rolled down for her. I reach over and scratch her behind the ear and she pretty much ignores me.

When the road goes from two lanes to four I start looking for a way to get off and then change my mind.

It's going in the right direction and right now there's not a lot of other cars on the road, so I decide to stay with it for a while. Might as well get some practice on these while there's not much going on. Frankie looks over at me for a second and then her nose is right back at the top of the window.

"So you really liked Abigail, didn't you, girl?" Frankie's tail thumps the seat a couple of times, but she doesn't look around.

"Yeah, me too," I say. "Never met anybody like her before. I bet if I hadn't come up on her when I did she'd have put that hammer through the truck window and dragged you out of there. Probably would have taken you home with her, too."

I can't tell whether Frankie's listening to me or not, which hardly ever happens. Usually she's looking at me or wiggling around or both, and now whatever she's smelling out there has all her attention. She's the same as me, I guess. Never been this far from home before. Used to be I always sort of knew what to expect, always had a place to be, and there was a time that it wasn't so bad, being at home. It's been a while, but I do remember. That gets me thinking about home the way it used to be, before we lost Frankie and Daddy got so bad.

"You would have liked him, girl," I say to Frankie. "My brother, I mean. Maybe better than you like me. Probably. Everybody liked Frankie."

She turns her head this time, probably because she hears her name, but goes right back to the window.

I'm about ready to start feeling sorry for myself about my dog liking Frankie best when I remember something. It wasn't true that everybody liked my brother.

Kenny. It takes me a minute to think of his name. It's been a couple of years since I've thought about him and longer than that since I've seen him. He never bothered me much, but for some reason he really didn't like Frankie.

I don't remember him until fourth or fifth grade; by then he was half a head taller than anybody else and mean as a snake. Mad all the time, and for some reason he picked Frankie to take it out on.

The worst year was when Kenny was in seventh grade. By then he was shaving and was strong as a bull. I think he worked with his daddy on their farm and it was mostly just the two of them, so he was out there in the fields a lot. He'd miss school in the fall and spring and they just sort of let him do it. I guess they knew what his home life was and how they were just barely making it. Like a lot of us. Thinking about it now, I wonder if his daddy gave him as much shit as mine gave me, and Kenny just brought it to school and passed it on down the line.

Like he did to Frankie. Frankie was always liked

by most everybody, even though he didn't have two nickels to rub together. Plus he was usually friendly, waving hi, laughing at everybody's jokes even if they were terrible, even teased the principal some, what was his name? Macintosh, that was it. Old Mac, everybody called him behind his back. Except one time Frankie was telling a story about him and called him that just about the time Old Mac was walking up behind him. Everybody got real quiet, and I guess Frankie figured out what was going on, because he said, like he didn't know the guy was standing right behind him, "I call him Old Mac because if I called him Baby Mac he'd really be mad," and the old man almost laughed out loud even though he was trying real hard to stay serious, and just turned around real quiet and walked away.

Kenny could never get away with anything like that, and he knew it. I don't know if he was in the crowd Frankie was talking to or not. Probably not, because everybody stayed away from him as much as they could. Anyway, he must have heard about it because everybody did. I know he heard it because a few days later he came up to Frankie at the lunch table and sat down right across from him. In about a minute they were by themselves at the table. Kenny had that look on his face and that way of, well, just being there that told people to stay the hell away. I wasn't even in the same part of the cafeteria when it happened, but Frankie told me all about it later.

"I hear you're Old Mac's favorite little boy," Kenny said.

Frankie didn't say anything. There wasn't anything anybody could say to Kenny when he was like that.

"I bet that's right. I bet you're his little boy. Old Mac's got a little boy all his own. He take you for rides in his car, I bet, and you do whatever he tells you to."

Old Mac was right behind Kenny by that time, and Frankie didn't look over at him, just said to Kenny, "You want to say all that again?"

Kenny got about one sentence into saying it all again when Old Mac tapped him on the shoulder. Frankie told me that Kenny jumped about a foot and when he turned and saw who it was, he leaned over toward Frankie and said, "I'll get you for this, you little shit."

Kenny was gone for four days suspension and after that he started skipping a lot of school, so Frankie never knew for sure when or where he was going to see him. As far as I know Kenny never caught Frankie out by himself, but it was always something Frankie had to keep in mind. All Kenny had to do was show up and you could see Frankie change, get more careful, look around more, that kind of thing. He never let on that it bothered him, but I

23

could tell. So I guess it wasn't true that everybody liked Frankie.

And of course I was too much of a damn coward to stick up for him.

I got to stop thinking about this kind of stuff. School is way behind me now and so is Kenny. Plus I'm not nearly as scared of shit as I used to be. I mean, I've been shot and knifed and got the scars to prove it. I touch the bullet scar and smile, and then start laughing out loud when I think about me and Gamaliel trying to patch each other up after he shot me.

One time when I stop to give Frankie a pee break I almost can't get her back in the truck. She's going crazy with all the new smells, plus somebody else in the parking lot has a dog on a leash, a little yippy thing that might have weighed five pounds soaking wet. Whatever kind of dog it is, it thinks it's king of something or other. When it sees Frankie it runs right at her, barking its head off, until it comes up to the end of the leash and almost lifts itself off the ground. Frankie wants to play, I can tell, but the other dog's owner is hauling away on the leash and heading back to his car as fast as he can, his dog fighting him every step of the way.

"Sorry, Frankie, no time for playing around," I say and get her back in the cab of the truck. The other dog's owner pulls out just ahead of us and is out of sight in less than a minute.

After we've been on Highway 74 for a while I see a drive-through hamburger place up ahead with some picnic tables off to the side under some pine trees. I get a couple of burgers and a large fries and the biggest drink they sell, which almost takes two hands. We find an empty table and I get Frankie's dishes out, tie her leash to the table leg, and sit down.

I'm about halfway through the second burger when a family pulls in and heads toward one of the other tables. They've got a dog, too, and the youngest kid takes him on a leash out under the trees. He heads over toward us and stops close enough so Frankie and his dog can check each other out. Lots of tail wagging and sniffing all around, and the kid grins. He's probably about twelve and kind of goofy looking, which I can sure relate to. I might not have been the worst looking kid in school, but I was a long way from the top of the list. He points toward Frankie and says, "What's her name?"

"Frankie."

He waves his hand at his dog. "This is Rocket."

Rocket is about Frankie's size, mostly white, and there's definitely some hound in there somewhere. He looks over at me and then goes back to bouncing around with Frankie.

I try to think of something to say and finally come

up with, "Nice looking dog. Had him long?"

The kid turns. "Hey, Dad, how long have we had Rocket?"

The guy gets up and comes over. "Afternoon. Name's Henderson." He sticks out his hand and I shake it.

"Boone. And this is Frankie."

He nods. "Nice to meet you. We got Rocket about four years ago. Shelter dog. Which way you heading?"

I shrug. "A friend of mine told me I needed to see the ocean, so I guess I'm going east. Never seen it before."

Henderson nods again. "Your friend's right, you know. Everybody ought to see the ocean at least once." He points to Frankie. "She's going with you, I guess."

"Sure." I think, what else would I do with her? I don't go anywhere without Frankie.

"Reason I ask, you know, is some beaches don't allow dogs."

I never thought about that. I don't want to drive all this way and then get told I can't go somewhere because of Frankie.

"Some do, though, right?"

He nods again. "There are some. I mean, you've still got to keep them on a leash, pick up the, you know, you have to clean up after them, but some beaches don't mind at all having dogs around. They advertise it so tourists will know, you know."

This guy sure nods and says you know a lot. I wonder if that ever gets on his family's nerves. It's kind of getting on mine.

"You know about any beaches I can go to, where Frankie would be okay?"

He nods and points down the road, same way I've been going. "You're not too far from Bolton, you know, and that's where 211 crosses 74."

"So what do I do when I get to Bolton?"

He drops his hand and turns back to me.

"You turn right on 211 and then right again on Long Beach Road. That'll take you down to Caswell Beach. It's not too far up this road, you know. The highway, not the beach."

I nod and think, damn, now he's got me doing it.

"Thanks. I appreciate it."

He nods and says, "Glad to help, you know." He waves his hand toward the other table. "That's my wife Kelly and our daughter Caroline. This is Clay," and he swings his arm around toward the kid, who still has Rocket on the leash, but they've left Frankie and are out in the trees. "We're on our way back from Caswell Beach, heading home to Asheville."

I don't say anything. My home is sitting right over there with the tailgate down. If he turns his head he'll be looking into my bedroom.

He stands there for another half a minute and

27

then nods. "You have a nice day, now." He starts back toward his family.

"You too," I finally say. "And, uh, thanks. Caswell Beach, right?"

He turns back and nods. "Yep. Nice place." Then he heads back to his family. They all get into the car and off they go, Clay waving to either me or Frankie from the back window. I watch them, thinking, we never did any shit like that when we were a family. Going to the beach, or going anywhere as far as that goes. I wonder if we would have gone anywhere if we hadn't been so damn poor or if Daddy was too mean to even think about it.

Guess I'll never know.

Chapter Three

After I turn onto 211 it's only about 45 minutes to Caswell Beach. I make the turn onto Long Beach road and after a while it sort of turns into Caswell Beach Road. The ocean is off to my right and after I go past a bunch of houses all lined up next to each other I see a big round building on the left. It takes me a minute to remember what it's called. Across from the lighthouse there's a parking lot so I pull in. I park and get Frankie on her leash and we walk along a kind of wooden sidewalk and then out onto the sand. We take about twenty steps out onto the beach and stop.

I've never seen anything like this. I mean, I've seen pictures, movies and all that, but this, I don't know how I feel about this.

The wind is blowing in from the ocean. I turn my face to it and then from side to side. There are a few clouds and I realize that I have no idea how far away they are because there's nothing out there to measure anything against. At home if something was farther away than the next hill or curve you couldn't see it. Here, everything is out in the open.

Off to my left there's something really big out on the ocean, way off, and I stare at it for a long time. It's blurry and I can't tell how far away it is because there's nothing anywhere around it, but I can tell it's really big. Somebody comes up behind me and stops right next to me. I point at the thing and say, "What the hell is that?"

The guy looks kind of puzzled and then says, "It's rain out on the ocean. You never seen rain before?" There's a girl with him and they both laugh and head on out across the sand.

I didn't drive all the way out here to be made fun of. I start to follow them out and tell him so, and then I think, the hell with it, Boone, you just got here and you're getting ready to pick a fight. Also, I'm watching them walk away from me and I notice a couple of things.

That girl is about as close to being naked as anybody I've ever seen and I wish I could see her from the front. From the back she looks pretty damn good.

The other thing is, I've got on jeans and a tee shirt and the only pair of shoes I own, and the guy is in a swimsuit and no shirt, and he's wearing flip flops. I can tell already that I don't fit in here. Course I'm used to that. I remember telling Tiny once that I didn't feel like I fit in and he laughed that short laugh of his and said, "Hell, nobody fits in, man. That's just the way it is."

Right now I want to go out at least as far as the water since I've come this far, so I take Frankie back to the truck and get in the back. I have four pairs of jeans altogether and one of them is about gone, so I get that pair out and my knife and cut them off above the rip that runs across my left knee. My shoes I leave in the back of the truck along with my jeans. I keep my t shirt on and step out barefoot onto the hot asphalt of the parking lot and get over to the sand as quick as I can.

The dry sand is kind of hard to walk on, even though Frankie seems to be doing just fine. It keeps giving way under my feet and I can't find any solid ground. About halfway to the water the sand gets a lot firmer and easier to walk on, and not nearly as hot. I stop a few feet short of the water and just stand there for a minute watching.

It won't keep still. That's the first thing I notice, and once that is in my head I can't stop thinking about it. Back home the land didn't move and even the water on the lakes would sometimes be smooth as glass. When I look way out the ocean kind of looks flat, but up close I can see that it's always moving, like it's alive or something.

"It's beautiful today, isn't it?"

I don't know why Frankie didn't let me know somebody else was there. I turn away from looking at the ocean and there are two people standing beside me about six or eight feet away. I look down at Frankie and she's sitting on the other side of me from these two still looking out at the water. I figure that means I don't have to worry much about whoever these people are. Frankie's been good about judging people, and I trust her. More than I trust, well, anybody.

"I mean, yesterday it was kind of cloudy and yucky and today the sun is out and the water's calm."

I shrug. "I don't know, just got here."

"I know." I look at her again and she's grinning and pointing to my legs. Her legs are the color of that leather bag that Nancy's mom used to carry with her, kind of a dark tan, and when I look at my legs and see how white they are I think about going back to the truck and getting a pair of jeans.

"Those legs haven't seen the sun much, have they?"

The other girl is grinning, too, and I'm starting to get pissed off. There's no reason for them to be making fun of me like that. I start to say something but the first girl, the one with the big floppy hat pushed back on her head, says, "We need to get some sun on those legs." She points off to the right. "Sully's back at the house, he's got a low country boil on the burner. It won't be long til it's ready, and we've always got room for one more. Why don't you join us, we'll start working on your tan while we're here, and it'll be time to go eat before your legs burn." She looks at my legs again. "I hope."

"Sure, I guess so," I say. I'm not sure what a low country boil is, but I'm not about to give them something else about me that they can laugh at.

We go about fifty or sixty yards along the beach and walk up to a group of about a dozen people, most of them about my age. I'm the only one with white legs, and a few people give me a look when we come up. Frankie is a big hit with everybody, as usual, and that helps get me past the first few minutes. Don't know what I'd do without her.

One of the guys there has a dog, too, a real beauty. She's black and white, mostly white, and after I'm there for long enough to get sort of comfortable he stands up and brushes off his suit and says, "C'mon, JJ, let's play," and the dog is up like a shot. He picks up a Frisbee and tosses it down the beach and JJ is up to full speed in about three steps. She jumps a couple of feet off the ground and snags the Frisbee out of the air and brings it right to Andrew, the guy who threw it. She's jumping around like, "Well, come on and throw it again!" and he does. JJ is under it way before it comes close to the ground, grabs it, and comes back at a dead run. They get into a rhythm and it looks like Andrew gets tired out first.

After a half hour or so the group breaks up and the girl that invited me says, "You're parked in that lot over there, right?" and she points to where the truck is. I nod and she says, "So are we. Just follow us back to the house and we'll eat as soon as we get there."

Turns out I really like low country boil. At least the part I recognize. There's some stuff in there that I've never seen before, but I see corn on the cob, and potatoes, and some kind of hot sausage, so I start with that stuff. It's easy to fill my plate with whatever I want because when we got to the deck where the burner sits, there's a long table covered in newspaper. A couple of guys pull a big strainer out of the boiling water and just dump it out on the table. Two other guys, Andrew was one of them, already had some tongs and spatulas and they spread the food out all along the table. Damn, it smells good.

The girl in the floppy hat grabs my arm. "I never introduced myself. I'm Jericho."

"Boone," I say, "and this is Frankie."

Jericho bends down. "Hello, Frankie!" She rubs Frankie's head. My dog is wiggling all over, loving every minute of this. Jericho straightens up and looks at my plate. "You need some shrimp and mussels, Boone. Here," and she grabs a pair of tongs and puts four or five shrimp in the middle of all my other stuff. They look kind of like the crawdads my brother and I used to catch in the creek, but bigger. She starts to put something else on my plate and I hold up my hand.

"Hold on, let me try to get through this first."

"You sure?"

"Yeah, this is a lot of food here."

It's really not, but I'm not sure about some of the stuff on the table. Hell, I don't even know how to eat it. I need to see somebody else do that before I make a damn fool out of myself in front of a whole bunch of people I don't even know yet.

Jericho shrugs her shoulders. "Okay, but all the good stuff'll be gone before you know it."

She wanders off when somebody yells, "Hey, Jericho, over here!" I look around, trying to figure out what to do next.

The closest I've ever come to this kind of thing was a long time ago, when the Thompsons used to have a big bonfire every now and then. They had hot dogs sometimes, and sticks to roast them over the fire, and they always had marshmallows. Some of the older kids would wander off into the woods after it got dark and come back laughing and whispering. We all knew they had some shine stashed back in the woods, but there was a kind of rule about who could go back and have a sip. I never did figure out what the rule was, and neither did Frankie as far as I know, but even without the shine it was a good way to get out of the house. We'd stay for hours, sitting around it until there wasn't anything left but a few coals. If we were old enough. I always had to leave before it was over and figured that I was missing out on all the good stuff, even though I had no idea what the good stuff might be. Anyway, I was never in with the popular kids, so even if I was old enough they would probably have shut me out. Funny that I ended up being such good friends with Tiny just a few years later. I barely remember him at those bonfires, but it was his family that put them on, so he must have been there.

When I look around I see that people are scattered all over the place. This is a really nice house. There's a picnic table underneath the deck where all the food is, and people are sitting there, and up on the deck, and on the stairs leading up to the deck. I look over at Frankie. "Come on, girl, let's find a place to sit down and I'll give you a couple of pieces of this sausage. When we get back to the truck I'll feed you again. Okay?"

I don't know who to sit with. Jericho is in the middle of a bunch of people, and I don't really know anybody else, so I just pick a spot and sit down. Frankie stretches out next to me and I'm about to start on the corn on the cob when I hear somebody say, "Here you go, girl, I brought you this."

I turn my head and Andrew is standing there with a big brown thing in his hand. He flips it to Frankie; it lands in front of her and she sniffs at it, picks it up in her mouth, and starts gnawing. Andrew looks over at me. "Pig's ear," he says. "Dogs love to chew on them."

Then he throws something at me. I barely catch it before it flies on past. It's a can of beer, some kind I've never heard of.

"You'll need something after you take a bite of that chorizo sausage," he says and laughs. "I'm going back to get my plate. Mind if I join you? JJ would love to hang out with your dog. Frankie, right?"

I nod.

"Okay. Back in a minute."

When he comes back he's not alone. Jericho is with him, and two more girls who act like they're in love with each other or something. I've heard about stuff like that but I thought it was made up. Guess not. It gives me a kind of creepy feeling, but I keep my mouth shut. Jericho sits down on the sand between me and Andrew and puts her plate in front of her. It's about to spill out all over the place. She picks up a shrimp and does this thing with her fingers real fast and the shell comes right off. She drops it back on her plate and puts the shrimp in her mouth, bites off the tail, and throws it down there

37

too. She looks over at me and grins and I realize that I've been staring at her.

"Want me to teach you how?" she says.

I start to say that I'm good, that I've done this lots of times, but then I think about how stupid I would look if I tried to do what she just did. So I nod.

"Like this," she says, and grabs, twists, and pulls, and the shell and legs are in one hand. The shrimp is in the other. She holds it out to me. "Here. This one came off your plate."

She snags another one from her plate. I try to watch what she does but it's awful fast. When she drops the tail and reaches for another one I realize I'm still holding mine, like a fool, so I do what she just did, bite the tail off and throw it on the pile.

By the time I get the hang of it I'm on my last shrimp. There's still a mostly full plate in front of me, though, so I start with the corn on the cob and work my way through the rest of the food. When I take my first bite of that sausage, whatever Andrew called it, I understand why he said I would need a beer.

All the food is really good, Frankie loves her pig's ear, and Jericho is really good looking. She's put one of those skirt things over her bathing suit, but if she's up and moving around and the sun hits it just right you can see through it, pretty much. Somehow that makes her even better looking. She catches me staring a couple of times, or maybe more than a couple, and one time I swear she smiles a little.

All in all, a good end to this part of the trip. I figure we've been in that truck for ten or twelve hours, doing all those side roads, so it's good to not have to think about getting back behind the wheel. I've never done that much driving before in my whole life.

Everybody is slowing down, seems like, just picking at their food. Andrew comes by with another beer and one for Jericho. "I'm all done," he says to everybody close by. "See you tomorrow. Come on, JJ," and he heads into the house. I hear a door close somewhere inside.

"Where are you staying?"

I turn and Jericho is looking at Frankie. Then she turns to me and raises her eyebrows.

I shrug. I really don't want to tell her I'm sleeping in my truck. It looks like somebody here's got money, with this nice house and all.

"Why don't you stay here tonight?"

Then she laughs out loud, I guess because of the look on my face. She's got a great laugh. She points to the door Andrew had gone through a few minutes before. "There's a couch in the living room, the first room you come to. Actually there's two couches, so you get your pick."

Chapter Four

The beach looks different because the sun's coming right at me, but, like yesterday evening, there's a strip of dry stuff that's really hard to walk on and then a strip that's wet, pretty smooth, and easy walking. That's where the people are, mostly, at least the ones who are moving. A couple of guys with dogs on leashes are running along the edge of the water, weaving in and out to stay out of the waves. The dogs are right beside them, which they have to do, I guess, because of how short the leashes are. Frankie's is a little longer than theirs, enough so that she's moving around, nose to the sand, trying to figure everything out.

It's hard to get a handle on all this. There's birds flying about a foot off the water a little ways out, just sailing along, and then one of them dives, I guess for a fish. A bunch of some other kind of bird is swooping around and making a hell of a lot of noise. Somebody shouts and points, and a couple of the biggest fish

41

I've ever seen are swimming along a ways out in the ocean, jumping and playing around. Little birds with long skinny beaks are running along right next to the water, back and forth. Frankie finds something moving on the beach and is heading toward it when I pull on the leash and stop her. It's a crab, a little tiny thing, running sideways across the sand with its claws up like it's ready to pick a fight with somebody. It's a lot to take in.

"Well, somebody's up early!" I turn toward the voice in case it's me they're talking to.

Andrew and JJ come jogging up, and JJ says hello to Frankie, tails wagging like crazy. Andrew puts his hands on his knees, breathing hard, and then straightens up. "That dog wears me out, but she loves a morning run."

I've never taken Frankie for a run, at least not on a leash. When I lived at Gamaliel's I'd just open the door and follow her out after a minute or two, maybe walk around a little while she was running after who knows what, and when I lived at the home I had to take her somewhere but there was always a place I could go and just let her off the leash. Not here. There's no place around that I know well enough to take the chance. I guess if I stick around for a while I'll need to do that, let her stretch her legs a little.

Then I remember that JJ wasn't on a leash last night when Andrew was throwing the frisbee.

"Frankie's not used to being on a leash," I say.

Andrew nods. "Yeah, JJ doesn't like it much either, but during the day all the dogs here have to stay on a leash. Even later on when we can let them off there's only a few places, and if we can't control our pets they'll make you use the leash all the time."

Man, I never had to worry about this kind of shit at home.

"Well," Andrew says, "I got to get moving. JJ needs exercise, and I probably do too." He looks at me like, are you coming?

"Okay," I say. "Have a good one."

Andrew shrugs. "See you around, I guess." He gives the leash a little pull and he and JJ head off down the beach. Frankie starts after JJ and stops when she gets to the end of the leash.

"Not today, girl," I say. "Let's just walk around a little. We got to decide whether we're going to stick around here or get out the map and go somewhere else."

Frankie is loving this place, even on a leash. She's in and out of the water, chasing the waves when they're going out and running as far as the leash will let her to get away from them when they come back in. For me it still feels pretty weird, no hills anywhere, and no trees either, just that grassy kind of stuff that grows in the sand. I feel like there's no place to hide if I need to, no place like the pool up above the house that nobody but me knew about. Lots of times when Daddy was really bad I'd go up there after he took off for work or wherever, and it made everything better, at least for a while. I guess I can see how the ocean could do that too, but there's no place here that's private.

We go back to the beach house before the afternoon sets in. It's hot as hell out on the sand and there's no shade anywhere, something else I kind of miss about home. Inside, both couches have people sleeping on them and all the bedroom doors are closed. I guess some of these folks don't like the sun either.

About five or six in the afternoon the rest of the crowd starts coming back from the beach and by seven or so everybody's here and talking about what to eat. One guy says we ought to go out to get some fresh seafood and Andrew says, "We just did that boil last night, man. I was thinking burgers and beer." It looks like most people want that, so Andrew starts collecting money from everybody. When he gets to me I ask him how much he needs, and he says everybody's putting in ten bucks, fifteen if you want to be sure there's enough beer. I dig in my pocket and pull out a twenty. It's all I've got left, but I tell him just give me five back and he does. "What kind of beer you like, Boone?" he asks me, and hard as I try I can't think of a single brand of beer.

"Whatever," I say. "I'll drink anything you bring back."

Andrew laughs and smacks me on the arm. "That's the spirit!" He finishes going around the circle and says, "I'll be back in twenty or so. Get the grill going, okay? And keep an eye on JJ."

That last part he says right at me, but Jericho, who is standing beside me, says, "No problem, Andy. Boone and I might take JJ and Frankie for an afternoon walk on the beach." She turns and gives me a wink.

Ten minutes later we're out of sight of the house and, since we turned right, on a section of beach I haven't seen before. She looks out to sea and says, half to herself, "Still early for hurricane season, but I don't like the look of those clouds over there."

I didn't even know hurricanes had a season. The only weather we cared about when I was growing up was mostly about enough rain for the crops and enough sun to dry the hay in the fields. Hay sure had a season, and so did tobacco.

The only time I ever had any money of my own growing up was hay season and tobacco season, and that was damn hard work. Hot sun, heavy bales, flies and dust and little pieces of hay all over all of us. When we got to the barns it was even worse, and when the weather was right we had to work our asses off before it rained and ruined it all. I was about half

45

mad and half glad when people started using those big round bales that you had to have a tractor to bring in. Less money for me, but hauling hay was nasty work. Tobacco was bad too, hot and sticky from all that sap, and those knives they used to cut the stalks were razor sharp and could take your finger right off if you weren't careful. A full stick was almost too heavy to lift, and if you got stuck up in the top of the barn hanging those sticks between two runners it was pure hell, having to balance one foot on each runner, reach down and grab the stick, lift and swing it into place, then do it all again over and over.

I remember one time we were hauling hay for some old guy, what the hell was his name anyway, and Daryl was sitting on the back of the trailer. He was the same age as me but he was trying to get in with the older guys and when they offered him a chew he took it. First time chewing tobacco, I'm pretty sure. He had a big mouthful of juice when the trailer hit a hole in the field and gave a big bounce. Daryl swallowed every drop of that juice and was sick as a dog for about half the afternoon. The older guys had a big laugh over it, and that was the last time Daryl ever tried chewing, as far as I know.

Daddy never knew how much I made doing that godawful work. He'd hold out his hand as soon as I walked through the kitchen door, and I always gave him about half of it. If he'd known I kept any for myself he would have given me a beating for sure, but he never caught on. One good thing about him being so drunk most of the time, I guess. His math wasn't all that good.

I feel a touch on my arm and look around.

"Boone, you were a thousand miles away just now. You okay?" Jericho is looking right into my eyes. "Because you were looking really sad and really angry all at the same time."

"Yeah, I'm fine. What was that you were saying about hurricane season?"

I don't feel like laying out my life story for her, or anybody else far as that goes. Some of it she wouldn't be interested in and some of it is nobody's business. And some of it, like what happened with Daddy, I'll never tell anybody. Ever.

Jericho looks at me for a second like she's waiting for me to say something else, and then shrugs and tells me about hurricane season, and how much damage they can do, and all that, and it makes me think that the mountains in Tennessee are a pretty good place to live, but I don't say that. Instead I say, "Where'd you get that name?"

"My parents, well really my mom, she was a fan of the old music, like way back in the 1970's," she says, "and there was this song that she really loved. She took the title and gave it to me for a first name. My middle name is Rebecca, after my dad's grandmother.

47

What about yours?"

"I don't have a middle name," I say, thinking how stupid was that to bring up names. Should have known she'd ask about mine.

Sure enough, she says, "Well, that's pretty unusual, but I was asking about Boone. Was that like Daniel Boone? That guy that lived way back in the, what, 1800's?"

I don't say anything for a minute and then I think, what the hell, I'll never see this girl again in my life, and so I tell her about Boone's Farm wine and my parents liking it a lot back then.

When I look over at her I can tell she's trying to be polite and stuff, but she can barely keep from laughing out loud. It makes me really mad for a second and I finally give it up and shrug my shoulders. "I know, I don't know whether to laugh about it or stay pissed off."

She lets out a long breath and grins at me. "I think laughing is better, don't you?"

She's right, I think, and so I grin back at her. "That's not something I tell everybody, you know?"

Jericho get this serious look on her face, nods, and says, "Very smart of you," and after a second we both start laughing. She turns around to head back and I watch her go, wondering whether she's already serious about anybody and realizing I don't have any idea how to find out. She turns and looks at me and it's like she's reading my mind. I stand there like a fool for a second and then hurry to catch up.

By the time we get back the burgers are on the grill and everybody's already got a beer in their hand. Andrew hands me a bottle that has something stuck in the neck. He sees me looking at it and says, "You push the lime down into the bottle as soon as you've got room. Mexican beer is great. Had any before?"

I shake my head and say, "Never even heard of it."

"So what do you drink where you come from?"

I tell him I'm from back in the Tennessee mountains, and I drink mostly moonshine. He looks at me like he thinks I'm full of shit, but all he says is, "Well, I hope you like this. It's pretty good stuff."

He's right, and the burgers are good, too. Frankie gets scraps from half of the crowd, and JJ works the other half, and they're both pretty happy about that. Later on that night, I take a quick look into the house, hoping that maybe I'll see Jericho, but she's nowhere in sight and both couches are full, with folks either asleep or crawling all over each other. I give it a few minutes and give it up. I'm guessing she and Andrew are back in one of the bedrooms and I won't see her until tomorrow, so Frankie and I go back out to the truck and spend the night there. I figure that tomorrow I'll decide whether to stick around or head out to one of the other places Melvin told me about back at the home. He sure made some of them sound interesting.

The next morning I'm sitting on the tailgate with Melvin's map spread out beside me when Jericho comes out of the house rubbing her eyes and looking around. She's got on an old faded out tee shirt that I think says, "Jamaica" on it and it looks like that's all she's got on, but it's kind of hard to tell. That makes her even better looking, not knowing for sure. She sees me and Frankie, wanders over, and looks down at the map.

"What are you doing, Boone? Why are you up this early? What time is it?"

I don't really know what time it is, besides morning. The sun is still pretty low over the ocean, so I guess it's early, but I don't know the exact time, so I don't say anything.

She squats down and says hi to Frankie, her shirt hanging open at the neck, and as far as I can tell what she's got on under it is nothing. She glances up and catches me staring.

"Like what you see?"

I can feel my face getting red and I'm trying to figure out what to say when she starts laughing.

"Don't worry about it, Boone. In case you hadn't noticed, we're all pretty casual here." She looks at me. "I know you've been checking me out. Kind of surprised you haven't tried anything. Are you gay?"

"Hell, no I'm not . . . you know, like that!" I'm

pissed off that she would even think that. I don't act like a queer, at least I don't think I do. Why would she ask me that?

She gets a really funny look on her face and doesn't say anything for a minute. "You know it wouldn't matter a bit if you were. Andrew is, and my friends Judy and Lania have been in a relationship for about a year now, ever since they came out."

There was this one guy at school, back before I stopped going, that everybody said was a homo. I know he got beat up a couple of times and made fun of almost every day. The seniors, and especially the ones in Mr. Timmons' gang, were out to get him for sure. That one time they came after me was nothing compared to how they treated that guy. I'm trying and can't even remember his name, but I know me and everybody else stayed as far away from him as we could. He was always by himself. I don't know anything about sex really, but when I think about it with other guys I get a little disgusted. I don't see how that works at all and don't much want to find out, so I'm sure I'm not gay. It does seem like they should have just left the guy alone, whatever his name was.

Troy, that was it. Wonder whatever happened to him. I look over at Jericho. She's standing up now, just looking at me.

"What do you mean, came out? Came out from

where?"

"You know, came out as lesbians. Wow, Boone, you really are from back in the hills, aren't you?"

Man, if I needed a reason to get out of here, I've got one now.

"You can make fun of where I'm from all you want to, you know, I really don't give a damn one way or the other. I'm out of here. Frankie, let's go."

I slam the tailgate shut and take Frankie around to the passenger door. When she's inside I close it and head around the front of the truck so I don't have to say anything to anybody. I just want to leave, fast as I can, before I say something even stupider than what I just said. I think I hear her say something but can't make out what it is. Doesn't matter much anyway.

I finally make my way back to 211, which is what I came in on, and when I get to 17 I turn left and start driving south. The morning sun is coming in on my side and the road stays close to the ocean. It takes me through some place called Myrtle Beach, which looks like it has about a million people and I get through as quick as I can. When I get to Georgetown I start heading west, away from the ocean.

I look over at Frankie. "So, girl, what did you think of the ocean?"

She doesn't answer, so I try again. "How about JJ?"

She thumps her tail a couple of times at that.

"I'm not sure how I feel, girl, to tell you the truth." I'm on 521 now, and I guess I should pull over sometime and look at the map. I start looking for a place and keep talking to Frankie.

"I guess I see why people like it so much, and I guess I'm glad Melvin told me I needed to see it, but I'm pretty sure it's not for me," I say. "I'm always kind of out in the open there and don't like that feeling. No place to hide, no privacy at all. Know what I mean, girl?"

Frankie keeps watching the world go by outside the glass.

"Now, Jericho, she was one fine looking girl," I go on. "If I wasn't such a damn fool I bet we could have done something," and that's where I stop talking because I don't know exactly what it is we would have done. I'll bet she knows what to do, which makes me think maybe it's better that nothing happened. She was already kind of laughing at me about the whole coming out thing, so I bet when she found out I'd never done it or even gotten close . . . .

Now I'm thinking about Jericho and Abigail and Nancy and it's all pretty depressing. I need to find something else to think about, so when I see an old abandoned gas station on my side of the road I pull into the parking lot and take Frankie out to pee and stretch her legs a little. When we get back to the truck I spread the map out on the tailgate and try to figure out where I am.

Looks like I'm coming up on a place called Manning, and that puts me right in the middle of South Carolina. Melvin has a few places marked—Savannah, Charleston, Jacksonville—but they're all on the ocean, and I feel like I've seen the ocean. Maybe I'll go back sometime, but right now I want something else. I'm just not sure what.

One place that might not be too far away is something called the Okeefenokee National Wildlife Refuge. I'm no good at figuring distances and times on the map yet, but I'm pretty sure it's less than a day away from here. I sit back and try to remember what Melvin said about it.

"It's like another world, Boone," he had said. "Swamps are mysterious, spooky, giant cypress trees and waterways down into the swamp and alligators floating with just their eyes showing. Not really my cup of tea, but a lot of people fall in love with it, how it soaks up the sound and how ancient it feels. Definitely going on the list," and he had circled it on the map and then tapped it with his pen. "You probably won't want to spend a lot of time there, but you really ought to see it."

"Why won't I want to spend a lot of time there?" I remember saying.

"As I said, it's like another world," Melvin had

grinned at me. "Makes some people uncomfortable."

When I remember that it pretty much decides for me where I'm going next. I got to see this swamp for myself. The beach was kind of another world already, and Melvin talked like it was just a neat place to go. Him saying that other world stuff about the swamp, well, I'm really curious now.

"Okay, Frankie, looks like we're headed south," I say. She's in the shade under the tailgate and doesn't answer. I bend over the map and start trying to figure out where to turn to get me pointed toward the swamp.

Chapter Five

When I get to Waycross, a guy in the gas station where I fill up the tank and get some cash from the ATM tells me that Highway 121 will take me to the east entrance to the refuge. He tells me how to get to the highway without having to go through town.

Using a machine in a gas station to get money is weird. Nobody else is close by, which is good, because I get my PIN wrong the first time and have to start all over. Plus it subtracts an extra $3.00 from my account for some kind of fee. I get $80.00, buy a couple of candy bars and three or four drinks, and head back out to the truck before somebody like Abigail comes along with a rock or a brick to rescue my dog.

Frankie is sitting in her seat waiting and thumps her tail at me when I climb in. I pull out of the station and head in the direction the guy said would get me to 121. We're in south Georgia now, which is a lot of pine trees and red clay, too flat to feel like home but more familiar than the beach. We get to Folkston and the east entrance to the refuge after about an hour drive and park at the visitor center.

I find out pretty quick that Melvin either didn't know or forgot about the rules here. Frankie isn't allowed in the canoes, which is no big deal, since I've never been in a canoe in my life and don't want to start in a place with alligators hanging around. She also can't go on the boardwalks, which is kind of a big deal, since a lot of the trails are boardwalks and that knocks out quite a bit of the park for us.

When I first got Frankie, and the whole time I lived at home, I never ran into any of this shit about not being able to take my dog with me. I mean, she couldn't go into the grocery store with me or anyplace like that, but if I hadn't run into that guy that told me about Caswell Beach I would have wasted a trip to the ocean, and now here I'm running into the same thing. Never thought of Frankie as a problem before; she's the best thing I've got going right now, and if there's a place she can't go then I don't want to be there either.

Course that's not entirely true. I'd like to have gone out on the boardwalks at least a little ways. Melvin was right about one thing. The swamp is like a whole different world, and I had to stand kind of on the edge of it to see what it was like. But I can't take Frankie except on the trails that are on solid land

and I'm sure not leaving her with some stranger just so I can go out into the swamp a little ways on one of the boardwalks.

I have to say, though, that being back in the woods, even though it isn't the same kind of woods I'm used to, feels awful good. I guess I'd forgotten what that's like. Then I think, it's been like a week, actually less than that, since you got on the road and you're homesick already. That's pitiful. I can hear Melvin saying, "You need to see some other places while you're young, Boone; you never can tell what will happen. You might find the perfect place to live or a vacation spot to keep coming back to, or maybe even the love of your life!"

He was grinning at me when he said that last part, I remember, because he knew about me and Nancy and was just giving me a hard time. He was a good guy; a lot of those old folks couldn't hardly remember their own name, but Melvin was pretty sharp.

By the time we get back to the truck from the two or three trails we can take, it's close to the end of the day and time to find a place to park and sleep for the night. I'm about to get in and head for the exit when I hear somebody yell, "Hey, Tennessee!" I don't think anything about it but then I hear it again and when I look around some guy's pointing at me and saying, "What part of Tennessee are you from?"

At first I don't say anything because I can't figure out how he knows that I'm from Tennessee, since I don't know him from Adam. He points at the license plate on the truck and says, "I saw your truck when we pulled in. Nice dog." He's walking over to us and Frankie is watching him. She's not doing anything, not growling, hair not standing up along her back, but she's not wagging her tail either. He gets a little closer and I can hear a growl, so low I almost miss it, but when I look down Frankie is all tensed up.

He's a big guy, not as big as Tiny, but big. He steps in way too close to me and Frankie's growl gets louder. I say, "You ought to step back a little. Getting kinda close there. Frankie doesn't like it and I don't much like it either."

"Maybe you ought to keep your dog under control," he says, and stays right where he is.

"She is," I say. "This is her being under control."

He stands there for a second, and then steps back. "I didn't mean anything by it." He raises his hands up in front of his shoulders. "Sorry." He doesn't look sorry.

"No problem," I say. "What can I do for you?"

He shakes his head. "Never mind, man, just trying to be friendly." He turns around and heads back to his car. There's two other guys there and I see him talking to them and pointing at us. They're too far away for me to hear.

One of the guys looks around the parking lot and says something to the rest of them. They all turn the same direction and look, so I turn that way too. I see a guy walking up to a big SUV. The first guy, the one who came up to me, says, "Hey, Virginia!" and the car owner stops and looks around the lot.

"Let's get out of here, Frankie," I say, and take her around to the passenger side. She jumps in and I start around the front, but when I look over at the SUV all three guys are standing around the driver almost shoulder to shoulder, and he's backed up against the rear fender of the car.

I never liked bullies; got pushed around plenty in school and couldn't do much of anything about it. Back then I knew nobody would back me up if I tried to stand up to them, especially Mr. Timmons' gang. If you don't have some kind of backup it's hard to stand up to anybody. That makes me think about Jerry and I reach up and touch the scar on my arm from the knife fight. Tiny stood with me then, and so did Nancy. I don't know whether these guys are bullies or thieves, but I've dealt with both kinds, and they both piss me off.

I'm trying to decide what to do about it when another car pulls in and parks one spot over from the SUV. Two people get out and the woman on the passenger side says, "When were you going to join us, Raymond? The grill's about ready." Then she looks at the three guys that have the driver, I guess that's Raymond, backed up against the car and says, "What's going on here?"

The one that had come over to me says something to her and she just stands there like she's not sure what to do. I can see Raymond's face enough to know he's scared, so I get Frankie back out of the truck and step out into the lot.

"Y'all okay over there?" I shout, and start walking toward them. Frankie is right beside me and I've got the leash wrapped tight around my hand. She's growling loud now, and when we get a little closer she barks once. Now she's pulling hard on the leash and everybody's looking at her. I'm wondering whether I should have gone into the back of the truck and picked up my shotgun when the three guys look at each other and start heading back to their car.

They get in their car and start to pull out of the parking lot, but turn in next to my truck on the passenger side. I can't really see what's happening but I hear glass breaking and then the car backs out, turns hard, and heads out of the lot. When I turn back around all three people, Raymond and the two others, are staring at me.

"I got the license number," the woman says. "Georgia plates. I'm going to call the police. Maybe they'll . . . ." She kind of trails off and looks at Raymond.

Raymond nods. "Maybe they will what, Denise? The police are not going to set up roadblocks for a broken window. Sorry," he turns to me and then back to her, "I say definitely call it in, but I would not expect anything to happen."

She nods and Raymond looks over at me. "I would like to thank you, young man. I do not know what would have happened had you not been here in the parking lot, but I am sure it would have been unpleasant at best." He holds out his hand. "My name is Raymond, as I am sure you have guessed by now. And who might you be?"

I grab his hand. He's got a solid grip. "Boone. This is Frankie."

Raymond smiles. "A great pleasure to meet both of you."

This guy talks like he's giving some kind of speech, even though it's just us and I'm sure he already knows Denise and whoever that other guy is.

Now he's calling them over. "Denise, Jeremy, come meet our rescuers. This is Boone, and this fine looking animal is Frankie." He looks at me. "With a name like Frankie, this could be either a male or female dog."

"Frankie's a girl," I say. I feel like I ought to do something besides just stand here, so I stick out my hand and we all shake, which feels weird because I don't ever do that. It's so serious, like we're making some kind of business deal or something. Then I say, "Frankie, this is Raymond, Denise, and Jeremy." She looks at the three of them and then back at me.

Raymond laughs. "Not easily impressed, is she?"

"She just doesn't know you," I say, not sure whether I'm supposed to get mad about that or not. "She's really a good dog."

"I have no doubt," he says. "Now, how shall we reward you? Aside from paying for a replacement window, I mean. Jeremy," he looks over at the guy, "Is your brother-in-law still working at his friend's body shop?"

Jeremy nods.

"Would you call him, please, and find out how much a replacement side window, parts and labor, would be? What year is your truck, Boone?"

I tell him and Jeremy steps away and pulls out a cell phone. He talks for a minute or two and comes back over.

"He says about $400.00."

Raymond nods. "Thank you, Jeremy."

"About what happened with those three assholes —" I stop and look at Denise. "Sorry about that."

She laughs. "No apology needed, Boone. I'd say that's exactly what they were."

"I didn't do anything besides walk over here. Those guys thought they had you cornered. They came at me just a couple of minutes ago, used that same trick on me they used on you. Backed off because they didn't want to have to deal with Frankie, so maybe she's the rescuer."

"Well said, Boone," says Raymond. "We will say both of you, then, since the two of you showed up together. Just in the nick of time, right?"

I shrug. "I guess so."

"Definitely so," says Raymond. "Now, you will join us for supper, of course. Where are you staying?"

Here we go again. I'm so damn tired of people asking me that. When I don't answer right away, Raymond takes the hint, I guess, and says, "No matter. We are in the RV park just outside Waycross. Did you come that way?"

I nod.

"If you will follow us, then, we will have a meal together, you can meet my wife Charlotte, and you can tell us about your travels with Frankie. Oh, I sometimes wish I was young again and able to just pick up and leave on a whim."

Denise laughs. "Ray, you're always picking up and leaving on a whim. I've known you for twenty years and this trip isn't new behavior for you." She glances at me. "You and Boone may have a lot in common, now that I think about it."

I don't know about all this, but I get in my truck and follow them out onto the highway anyway. I hope this doesn't turn out like it did with Jericho.

65

We're behind Raymond's car and Jeremy is out ahead a little ways. Denise had said something about getting the steaks on the grill as soon as they got there so we wouldn't be too late eating. Raymond drives pretty fast for an old guy and I have to pay attention so he doesn't get away from me.

There was this family back home, the Binfields, that had a house set so it looked out on the valley one over from us. You could see that place from anywhere, especially late in the day when the sun hit all those windows. I remember Daddy used to say those people had enough money to burn a wet dog, which I thought was pretty damn funny until I got Frankie. Anyway, that family was richer than anybody else in the county.

I don't think Raymond has that much money, but he's sure got a nice RV.

Chapter Six

The campground is more like a parking lot in the woods. The little roads that wind around through the trees have open spaces on both sides with picnic tables, grills, and places to park whatever you came in. I see a couple of trucks set up like mine but a lot nicer, and everything else is really fancy. Raymond pulls into a spot and I crowd in beside him, taking up the last open slot at his campsite.

I can barely get the door open, but I squeeze out and get Frankie from the other side. There's the two I saw at the swamp, so with my truck there's three cars crowded in next to one of the biggest RVs in the campground.

Raymond is waving me over to the picnic table. He's standing next to a woman who I guess must be Charlotte. I'm pretty sure that's what he said his wife's name was, and he's got his hand on her shoulder. They look like they belong to each other. Somebody told me once that people that have been married a long time start to look alike, and I guess that's true, even though I'd never noticed it. Momma and Daddy didn't have that much time together, and besides, they wouldn't ever stand together like that. I remember once Momma was at the stove and Daddy walked over to her. He brought his hand up and set it on her shoulder and you could see her flinch and tighten up.

"Boone, may I present the love of my life, Charlotte. Charlotte, this is Boone, the young man who rescued me from an extremely unpleasant situation. Oh, and this is Frankie." The woman smiles and holds out her hand.

"It's a pleasure to meet the two of you," she says. "I'm so glad you will be joining us tonight. I hope you like steak. We were just ready to pull Ray's off the grill. He prefers his rare. How about you?"

We didn't ever have steak at our house, so I don't really know much about how I like mine. There was that one time that Momma found some in the section where they sell stuff that's about to go bad. She fried it up and we each got a little piece. It was pretty hard to chew but it was okay with a lot of ketchup on it.

"Rare is good," I say, mainly because I don't know what else there is. She's still holding on to my hand and lets it drop so she can pet Frankie. She lets Frankie sniff the back of her hand and then scratches her behind one ear.

"What a fine dog," she says. "What breed is she?"

When I tell her I'm not sure, that she was the runt of a litter that a friend of mine was giving away, and that he was about to toss her in the river because she was so small and he figured nobody would want her, Charlotte shakes her head. "It's a good thing you saved her, Boone. She looks like she's turned out well."

"She did," I say. "Didn't you, girl?" Frankie's got her nose in the air checking out all the new smells and doesn't answer.

Raymond says, "I saw you eyeing our home on wheels, Boone. Would you like a tour while they finish the steaks and . . . ." He turns to Charlotte. "What are we having with our steaks?"

"Not much, I'm afraid. We're grilling some corn on the cob and there'll be a bowl of raw veggies on the table. You know, carrots, celery, little tomatoes, and sweet peppers with two kinds of dip. I think we'll have ice cream for dessert."

Raymond frowns. "We should have something more elaborate since we are entertaining guests."

"I'm good," I say. "Sounds like a great meal." Actually it sounds like the best meal I've had in a long time. I mean, the seafood stuff was okay, but this sounds like the kind of food I already like. The only thing is, I'm not crazy about raw vegetables, but at least I know what they are. Dip for vegetables

69

sounds weird, though. Dip is for chips and stuff like that, like they used to have up at the Thompson's bonfires.

One thing Melvin said was that I needed to try out at least one new food everywhere I visited. "It'll help you remember the place when you get back home," he had said. "There are some delicious meals out there you can't get around here." Then he had started talking about Maine lobster and New Orleans gumbo and Memphis ribs, and I remember getting hungry just hearing him talk about it. I'm not sure what kind of food I need to try from the swamp, but Raymond's offer sounds really good.

It turns out to be better than I thought it was going to be. We don't get a chance to do the tour before we eat, which is okay because I am starved to death. Raymond gets out a bottle of wine and pours a glass for everybody. I never had red wine before and it tastes kind of bitter, not as bad as the first batch of shine that Tiny and I tried to make after Gamaliel was gone, but pretty strong. Raymond says that a steak like we're having needs a strong red, but I don't know anything about stuff like that. I watch everybody else and they take really small drinks in between bites of steak, so I do that too. It's really good, the steak and wine together, and Charlotte passes around some stuff that looks kind of like mayo and she says is aioli. The others are putting it on

70

their corn, which I think is weird until I try it.

At the end of the meal Denise brings out a carton of vanilla ice cream and some chocolate sauce to pour over it. It makes me think of the volcano that Nancy and I split that one time; this is just plain compared to that, but it's still a good way to finish everything off.

Raymond lays his hand on Charlotte's and says, "Excellent as usual, my dear," and she gives him a smile. I'm thinking they might as well be by themselves instead of with the three of us and Jeremy must be thinking the same thing.

"Want us to leave you two alone for a while?" He and Denise both laugh and Charlotte blushes a little bit. Raymond just grins, but he does take his hand off of hers. He swings his legs around. stands up, and heads into the RV; he's back out again in a half a minute with a jar in his hand.

"I purchased this in Atlanta two days ago," he says, and sets it down in the center of the table. "Genuine moonshine from the hills of Tennessee." He looks over at me. "Have you sampled moonshine before, Boone?"

I think about me and Gamaliel sampling that first batch we made together and all the other times we sat in that back room sipping and talking about nothing in particular, and Raymond puts his hands on the table and leans across to me.

"And what are you smiling about, my friend?"

Before I can say anything Frankie nudges me in the side and I say, "I have to take her for a little walk. Be right back."

Raymond nods. "There's a place at the back of the loop that does not have any campers occupying it. You can walk a short distance into the woods from there if Frankie is looking for a private place."

I'm thinking while we walk back along the road that Frankie doesn't care about privacy at all. She just does her business wherever. This time after she's finished I get one of the little plastic bags out of the holder and clean up. I'm getting pretty good at this; the first time I had to clean up her dogshit I couldn't figure out exactly how to get it in the bag without getting it all over my hand, and then realized that if I put it on kind of like a glove and then turned it inside out I could tie everything up and toss it in a trash can.

There's a building on the way back, kind of in the middle of all the campsites, with bathrooms and showers. I stop there to throw away the bag and give my hands a quick rinse.

When I get back Raymond is sitting at the picnic table with the moonshine and two glasses. "The others decided to take an after-dinner stroll around the camp," he says, "so you and I have a chance to chat a bit. How do you take your moonshine? I assume from your smile earlier that this is not your first taste."

I slide onto the bench opposite him and say, "My friend Gamaliel would shoot me if he heard I put anything in the glass except shine."

"Now that is a name one does not hear often," he says. He pours a little in the bottom of the glass and hands it to me, pours one for himself, and raises his glass to me. I hold mine up too and he leans forward, taps my glass with his, and says, "Cheers!" He drinks it down in one swallow and I do the same, except what I want to do is spit it out on the ground. It's got some kind of fruity taste to it.

"What do you think?" asks Raymond.

"Tastes like fruit," I say. "I didn't expect that."

"You do not approve," he says. "It is plain from your expression. My apologies."

He starts to put the lid back on the jar. It's in some kind of jar like they use for canning beans and stuff. I push my glass back over to him. "Let me try that again, if you don't mind. Now that I know what's coming, I mean."

He smiles and says, "Certainly. I was afraid I had offended you in some way. Certainly you may try again, and I believe I will join you." He pours again, a little more this time, and says, "Here's to Gamaliel," raises his glass, and I raise mine again.

The second one is easier, but this is not the real

thing. I don't know whether to tell him or not, but I feel like he's gotten ripped off. The stuff Gamaliel and I made was a lot better.

"So, Boone, tell me about him," Raymond says.

I set my glass down, close enough for him to put a little more in if he decides to. "He used to live next door to us when I was growing up. Nobody ever saw him, he was old and kept to himself more than most. Anyway, I needed to borrow a bicycle pump one day and his house was the closest one."

Pretty soon I'm telling him all the stuff I can remember about the old man, from the lottery ticket to the still up behind my house to him accidentally shooting me, all the way up to the funeral, and Raymond doesn't say a word. One time he pours another drink, a strong one this time, and pushes it over in front of me. I'm mostly looking at either the table top or at Frankie while I'm talking, and when I look up Jeremy and Denise and Charlotte are all standing behind Raymond.

I pick up the glass and this time I'm the one that says, "Here's to Gamaliel," and Raymond and I touch glasses and drink one for the old man. Even though he'd never drink this fruity shit.

Nobody says anything for a long time and then Charlotte says, "What a beautiful story and a beautiful friendship the two of you must have had. Gamaliel reminds me a little of your father, Ray,"

74

and she looks at him sitting there staring off into space. He shakes his head a little and nods. "I was thinking the same thing, my dear."

He looks across the table to me. "My father did not suffer fools gladly. If you could count yourself a friend of his, you were a member of a very small, very select group. I believe my dear wife is correct in seeing the similarities between my father and your friend. Gamaliel must have seen something in you, young man, to allow you into his life. Something genuine and worthwhile."

I don't know what that whole suffering fools thing is about, but if he means that Gamaliel didn't like people who tried to make themselves all important and shit then he was absolutely right. He's wrong about one thing, though. He's wrong about me. I don't put on just to make people think I'm something, so he might be right about the genuine part.

Not the worthwhile part, though. I don't know a lot, but I know what I am. I've been white trash all my life, and I don't figure that's going to change anytime soon. There's still a lot of Daddy in me, and that's not something you just set down and walk away from. Much as I'd like to.

All this gets me thinking about Nancy. I never understood why she picked me out from everybody else. At first I figured it was because she felt sorry for me, like I was some kind of project. Helping the handicapped, that kind of shit. That sort of pissed me off and I kept waiting for her to drop me or pull some kind of joke with all her friends. I figured I'd never see it coming.

She never did, though, and if it wasn't for Stan it might have turned into something. I don't know about that, but I do know I was this close to getting into her pants. That time at the old folks home after the fire, if Frankie hadn't interrupted us it might have happened right then. Just that by itself would have made it worth it if she had turned out to be playing some kind of game on me. I've been made fun of plenty of times. Definitely would have been worth it.

I'm pretty sure that's all gone now. Even if Stan eased up on her she's probably not thinking about me or anything else besides starting college and getting out of her house. That was one thing. She had all kinds of stuff I wouldn't ever have, but both of us had pretty shitty home lives. They weren't the same but they were both bad.

Raymond is talking but I miss the first thing he says. When I start paying attention he's saying, "Our young friend is apparently lost in memory. Would any of you care to join us? We have moonshine left to share, even though it is substandard according to Boone's palate." He gives me a wink and turns back to the others. "Any takers?"

76

Jeremy and Charlotte are shaking their heads, and Denise sees that and says, "Well, I guess it's up to me to keep these two in line." She looks around for a glass and doesn't see one. "Be right back."

Charlotte pats Raymond on the shoulder. "Jeremy and I will be in the RV, dear. There's a movie I've been dying to see and I know you're not interested in character studies."

"Only if it is your character, my dear," Raymond says, and she sighs.

"Watch out, Boone. My husband tells the most outrageous lies when he has a glass in his hand." She looks over at Denise, who is sliding in beside me. "Keep an eye on him for me, will you?"

Denise turns to me. "We'll do what we can, right, Boone?"

I don't know what to say, because I'm not used to people joking around like this. If this is joking. I don't think they're mad at each other, but I can't tell because I can't keep up with this kind of shit.

Denise slides her glass over to Raymond. "I'm way behind here, Ray, so I need to get started." She rattles the ice cubes she put in the glass when she was inside.

Raymond looks at me. "Should we tell her?"

I shrug. "It's okay. I had to put ice in it and mix it with Thunderstorm for Nancy the first few times."

"Very well, then," Raymond says and pours

77

enough into Denise's glass to float the ice cubes. "Shall I refresh yours, Boone?"

That probably means do I want some more, so I nod and hand him my glass. He holds up the jar like he's calculating something and then pours a small drink for me and one for himself.

The rest of the evening goes by pretty fast. Charlotte comes out once and says they're halfway through the movie but she doesn't stick around more than a couple of minutes. Raymond doesn't ask me any more about Gamaliel, which is good because I've told him pretty much everything except about the box of money and I'm not saying anything about that. He starts talking about a trip he took when he was younger, "Not much older than you, Boone," he says, and how he slept in the back seat of his car and just drove around until the money he took with him was half gone. Then he turned around and headed back toward home, going a different way so he could see more. That makes me feel a little better and I think if he asks me again where I'm staying I'll just point to the truck.

About an hour after Charlotte, Jeremy comes out with a glass of water and a bottle of pills in his hands. He sets them down in front of Raymond and says, "The movie's over and Charlotte is going to call it a night. She says take your medicine before you turn in. I'm going to watch whatever kind of local news they have here and then I'm done, too." He looks over at Denise. "What about you?"

She shakes her glass and says, "I'm about fifteen minutes away from heading inside. Catch you at the end of the news."

He nods and goes back to the RV.

Denise shakes her head. "He always was a lightweight. If the sex wasn't incredible I'd never have married him."

"Yes, about that," says Raymond. "You might want to consider lowering your volume while we are on this trip together and sharing such a confined space."

He glances my way. "I would offer the extra bed to you, young man, but you might not get a full night's sleep." Then he and Denise start laughing and it's like they can't make themselves stop.

The last time I remember feeling like that was before Frankie died. He could get us all laughing around the kitchen table and Momma would be wiping her eyes and Daddy would get this big grin on his face. It was great.

And then it all disappeared. Just like that. We never got over his death. I think it killed what little bit of family we had, losing Frankie like that.

Now I'm mad at Daddy all over again for being such a cheap bastard that he wouldn't let Momma take Frankie to the doctors until it was too late. I know it tore him up something awful, what happened to his favorite kid, but right now I don't even care.

Raymond and Denise are settling down some and I stand up. "I ought to take Frankie out one more time before it gets too late." I start toward the same place I took Frankie before and Denise says, "I might be inside when you get back, so, goodnight, Boone. See you tomorrow morning?"

I shrug. "I hadn't thought about tomorrow yet. You have a good night."

She looks at me kind of funny and says, "Well, okay then. Goodnight."

Frankie and I turn toward the road and Raymond says, "Memories are difficult sometimes, are they not?"

He gets up and walks over to where we're standing. "Do you mind if I accompany you? I could do with a short walk to stretch my legs before I retire."

"It's okay with me," I say.

We step into the road together and start walking. Nobody says anything for a few minutes.

"Will you be moving on tonight, then?"

I glance over at Raymond, but he isn't looking at me. He's looking at Frankie, and she wags her tail at him.

"She is a fine animal, Boone. The two of you are well suited for each other."

"I don't know what I'd do without Frankie," I say.

This is weird. I don't hardly know this guy at all, and it kind of feels like I'm talking to Mark back at the home. He never has said what he does for a living, so I guess he might be a preacher, but I don't really think so. It gets quiet again, and after a minute I try to figure out what to say to him and finally come up with, "So, are you on vacation?" which as soon as I say it I think is stupid, because he's driving around in a big RV. Of course he's on vacation.

Raymond smiles. "I think you might consider me on an extended vacation. You are curious about the RV, I take it?"

I shrug. "It's pretty fancy."

He laughs out loud. "Yes, it is that. A trifle ostentatious, but there were things that I wanted and things that Charlotte wanted and by the time we put the two lists together we ended up with what you see back there."

He looks at me. We're standing in the middle of the road, just standing, but it's late and there's nobody else around. "You are curious about how I can afford something so extravagant but are too polite to ask."

Well, he's right. I am curious, but that might be the first time anybody's called me polite. He waits just a second and then starts talking again.

"I was one of those fortunate persons who was in the right place at the right time, with the right set of skills. I know a little about computer programming, and several years ago I was working for a company that shipped goods of various kinds all over the country. The method they used to keep track of their trucks and what was in each, whether they were on schedule, if there was a way to carry a full load in both directions, and so on was hopelessly antiquated, but they were bound by habit. I spent some of my own time, actually quite a lot of my own time, creating a program that increased their efficiency dramatically and saved them money in several other ways. I had created it and copyrighted it myself, and it could be used in many types of businesses. I lease the program to them and half a dozen other firms and the income allows me to travel in comfort."

I understand about a tenth of what he says, but I get the general idea. "So you're retired?"

Frankie gives the leash a tug and we start walking again.

"The term retirement has a negative connotation I am not comfortable with, Boone. Let us say instead that I am no longer doing the work I used to do, and the next thing has not suggested itself."

"You don't have to do anything, though, right?"

I'm still working on this idea, that he can just wander all over the place. I've never known anybody like that, ever. Course I don't know that many people.

"Let me ask you a question, young man. If you had the money to do nothing, how long do you think you could do that before you started looking for something to occupy your time?"

When I don't answer after a minute, he says, "I think you are too smart and self-reliant to spend your life sitting, doing nothing, even if you could. I think you would find a way to be useful in fairly short order." He clears his throat and says, "Enough of this philosophical monologue, I think. I may have too much moonshine in my system to indulge in such a serious topic for long. I fear I will start babbling soon."

That's okay with me. What I want to do right now is get Frankie taken care of and crawl into the truck. It's been kind of a long day, and even though I like Raymond okay I'm about ready for a break. All I really wanted to do back at the parking lot was get those assholes to leave him alone. It wasn't any big thing I did.

Chapter Seven

The next morning there's a lot of people in this RV park that are up early, cooking on grills and bicycling around, stuff like that, so it's a little noisy. Nothing like waking up beside the highway that first morning of my trip, though. I take Frankie out for a walk and end up talking to an old couple who are out walking a dog that looks like it's all hair. It's barking up a storm at Frankie until the old woman tells it to hush up, which it does right away. Frankie isn't much interested in the little thing, and we end up walking part of the way around the loop together. They're from some place in Colorado and are heading toward Savannah. Their favorite place on their trip so far, they tell me, has been New Orleans. That was one of the places on Melvin's list, so I say, "How come it was your favorite?"

"Oh," says Gail, "the way they came back after Katrina, mostly. We really didn't know what to expect when we got there, and in a lot of ways it felt like it did when we were there before the hurricane."

I didn't know who Katrina was when she started talking, but now I remember something, maybe. I was probably eight or nine, so I'm not even sure about that.

"A friend of mine tells me there's good food there," I say. I don't know if I'll ever make it there but I might. It's one of the circles on Melvin's map.

That gets them going and they spend the rest of the time we're walking telling me about blackened fish and dirty rice and something I've never heard of they call a ben-yay.

"You cannot go to New Orleans without going to the Cafe Du Monde," says Daniel. "Beignets are their speciality. Be prepared to stand in line for a while, and get a cup of coffee to go with them. It's almost worth the trip just for that."

They make me promise to get a beignet when I go and then say they are going to cut across the loop and get back to their RV. That little hairball of a dog starts barking again while they're walking away, but Frankie can't be bothered with it.

By the time I get back to Raymond's RV people are outside sitting around the picnic table. Charlotte has a plate of fruit, which I think is weird for breakfast, and when I come up she says, "Oh, good, Boone, you're just in time. We have fruit, granola, and yogurt if you want a topping. The honey is for the toast that Ray is about to bring out, but I suppose it could go on other things as well. How do you take your coffee? Or would you prefer hot tea?"

I tell her coffee is fine and sit down next to Jeremy. He's got a bowl of something that kind of looks like cereal which I guess is granola and he's putting big globs of white stuff on top and then mixing it in. I'm thinking I might just have a piece of toast and some coffee.

Raymond comes out and hands around plates, then deals out the toast. I put a lot of honey on mine even though I'm used to just butter and maybe some grape jelly. There's strawberries on the big plate in the middle and I grab a couple of those. When I look up Charlotte is standing next to me with a cup, ready to pour me some coffee.

I tell her I like it black and she hands me a full cup. The breakfast is really good, even though there's no biscuits or fried eggs or jelly for the toast. I finish up quick and go over to the truck to make sure Frankie has food and water, and Raymond comes over and stands beside me. He hands me a card and an envelope and says, "That is my cell number, Boone. We are getting ready to leave, maybe as soon as we finish breakfast, and I would like to stay in touch with you if I can. There is $500.00 in the envelope. We do not know what the cost for the window will be, but that should cover it." He just stands there like he's waiting for something, and I finally figure it out.

I haven't even looked at my phone for a day or two. I get it out of the glove compartment and look at the little piece of paper I put in there with it. I don't even know my own number. I tell him and he writes it on another one of those cards.

"Very good," says Raymond. "I will certainly call on you and Frankie if I should need another rescue."

I don't like how this feels. I just met the guy yesterday but it seems like I'm saying goodbye to somebody I've known for a long time. "Me, too," I say, and he laughs and after a second I start laughing with him. He sticks out his hand and I grab it.

"Safe travels to you and Frankie," he says. "I have to begin the process of packing up the RV and hooking up Denise's car. We usually drive one car and tow one, and take turns riding in Big Blue." I figure that's the RV.

"Same to you, Raymond," I say. "And thanks for the meal. It was awful good."

I find a place to park the truck close by so I can watch them leave. Charlotte is behind the wheel of Big Blue and she pulls it out far enough for Denise to get her car in behind it. Raymond and Jeremy hook it up to the back end and Denise gets in the other car with Jeremy. Raymond looks around, sees us standing by the truck, and gives us a wave. Then he disappears inside the RV and they pull out slow. In just a minute or two they are around the circle and ready to pull out onto the road. They're heading back toward the swamp, but I figure they're going to pass it by and go on to wherever's next on their list.

Jeremy pulls his car in next to mine and hands me a piece of paper out the window. "I looked around on the internet and found a place on the other side of Waycross that can put a new window in this morning. You might need to wait a bit since you don't have an appointment, but they said they could squeeze you in."

I take the paper from him. "Thanks, man, I appreciate it."

"No problem," he says, and waves goodbye. They head out to catch Big Blue and I look at the paper. It's a map one of them drew, and it looks like a straight shot past Waycross and a couple of turns will get me there.

The guy in the office says it'll be a half hour or maybe a little more before they can get to me, so I park where he tells me to and start to leave, figuring I can just walk around with Frankie for a while.

"Keys," he says.

I turn and look at him.

"Need your keys so I can pull the truck into the bay," he says, and holds out his hand.

I start to tell him no way in hell am I giving you

my keys and then I figure out the only other choice is to sit in the tiny little room with him until they're ready for me. I don't even know if Frankie could stay in there with me, so I say, "Let me get my phone out of the truck and I'll bring them back to you."

He shrugs and I go out, grab my phone and the envelope that Raymond gave me, look around to see if there's anything else I need to take, and stick my head back in the office. I toss him the keys and he says, "Want me to text you when we're done?"

"No," I say. "We're just going to walk around right close by. I'll keep an eye out for when you move the truck."

It's more like an hour before the truck goes into the shop, but it's a pretty quick job once they get it in there. When they pull the truck back out into an empty space, I go into the office and pull out the envelope.

"How much do I owe you?"

The guy shakes his head. "Nothing. All taken care of. You're good to go."

Damn. I didn't expect that.

I take the key from him and tell him thanks for working me in. Frankie and I get in the truck and before we pull out into traffic, I open the envelope. There's a bunch of bills in there, and a note. I put the envelope back in the glove compartment and say, "Let's find a place where nobody will bother us,

Frankie. Looks like Raymond left me some kind of note."

We had passed a church on the way to the shop and I'm not real sure what day of the week it is, but I remember the parking lot being empty, so I turn back the way we came and pull into the church lot. There's a big tree toward the back and I stop under the shade, even though it's not too hot yet. I give Frankie some water and a little food to keep her busy, sit on the tailgate, and open up the envelope.

When I count the money it comes to $500.00, just like Raymond said. It seems like a big reward for just running those guys off that were hassling him in the parking lot, especially since he also paid for my window, but I guess he's got a lot of money and this isn't all that much to him. It's a lot for me, though.

The note isn't from Raymond. It's from Charlotte.

My dear Boone,

After he came to bed last night Ray couldn't stop talking about you. You made quite the impression on him, and he doesn't impress easily. I'd like to thank you for giving my husband an evening of such pleasant companionship. I'm sure there are times he wishes he was out on the road in a pickup truck instead of this monstrosity we tool around in, so he's probably a little jealous of you and Frankie.

Safe travels to you and your fine dog, and if you're ever up in the Shenandoah Valley in Virginia, please stop by for a visit. We would both love to see you. We're just north of Staunton, in the middle of the state. You are welcome anytime, as long as we aren't on the road somewhere.

Thank you again and take care of yourself and Frankie,

Charlotte

I wonder if Charlotte was the one that paid the bill at the shop. I figured it was Raymond when the guy told me I didn't owe anything, but I look at this note and think maybe it was her. It's funny, because we never said much to each other. Makes me wonder why she would lay out all that money for somebody she didn't even know day before yesterday.

"Guess they've got it to spare," I tell Frankie, even though I don't have any idea what it's like to have money to spare. Everybody I know, if they get a little money they hang on as tight as they can.

I get out Melvin's map. I figure while we're sitting here in the shade we might as well think about where to go next. It takes me a minute to get the map unfolded and find Waycross again, and when I do I put my finger on that spot and just look at the map for a while. I'm trying to remember what Melvin said about some of these places he circled.

There's a whole bunch of the country he didn't do anything with, and that's okay with me. I'm already feeling like I'm pretty far away from home, so Colorado, where that old couple is from, and California, and all those other places might as well not be out there, at least as far as this trip goes.

"Maybe next trip I'll buy my own Big Blue and take off out West," I tell Frankie. "What do you think about that, girl?"

I finally decide to head west, figuring if I don't decide anything before I get to the Mississippi River I'll either turn left and go to New Orleans or right and go to Memphis. Maybe New Orleans; that old couple made those beignets sound pretty damn good. Anyway, all I have to do now is pick a road that goes west and stays out of Atlanta. One time after Nancy took me to Market Square to see that blues band, I was complaining to somebody about the traffic. I remember he said, "You think that was bad? Atlanta is ten times worse and it's that way twenty-four seven."

So Atlanta is out.

Looking at the map, starting from Waycross it looks like Highway 84 runs more or less west and after a while puts me a little south of Jackson,

Mississippi. I can start heading that way and if nothing else comes up by the time I get to Jackson I can decide about going north or south from there. I fold up the map and tell Frankie what we're doing. She's agreeable, but then she almost always is. Frankie is easy to travel with, except I have to do all the driving.

After we find 84 and settle in, I start thinking about all that stuff Raymond was saying last night. A lot of it I didn't understand then and I still don't, but I get that he's okay with just hanging out and waiting for the next thing to show up. Now that I've got this envelope full of money I guess I can do that too.

"Hey, Frankie," I say. "We should look for another rich guy to rescue and see what kind of reward we get. How about it?"

The thing is, I didn't know I was rescuing Raymond from anything, and I didn't know he had money. So that's not really much of a plan.

We spend the day following 84 toward Jackson. I think it's probably going to take all day to get there and we could make the trip a lot quicker on the interstate, but I don't like to drive on the interstate. Besides, I'm not in any real hurry. So Frankie and I drive and talk about Raymond and Charlotte and Jericho and JJ and Abigail.

"I think on our way back we need to go by the Ocoee, Frankie," I say. "Maybe we'll run into Abigail."

Frankie's tail thumps the seat and she looks around for a second before going back to the open crack at the top of the window.

I don't know exactly why she got to me, but she sure did. I mean, Jericho is a lot better looking than Abigail; of course I never got to look down Abigail's shirt, so I don't know that for sure. Jericho, except for that last thing she said about me being from back in the sticks, was really nice to me. Abigail mostly gave me shit. So what is it about her? I don't know. She keeps popping into my head.

"I'll have to tell her about those three assholes that smashed the same window she was planning to break when she was about to rescue you," I say. Frankie looks over at me and whines, which usually means she needs to find a place to squat.

"Okay, girl, I'll start looking," I say, and after about a mile and a half there's an old building, looks like it might have been a restaurant once, and a parking lot that's got weeds growing up through the pavement in a few places. I pull in and stop away from the road, get out, and get Frankie's leash.

She definitely needed to stop, and I decide to walk her around for a few minutes after she finishes. Not sure exactly where we are, but I know we're out of Georgia, so this must be Alabama. Unless we've already crossed into Mississippi, and I don't think we have. We haven't been driving that long.

I'm about to put her in the truck and get back on the road when a police car pulls into the parking lot and stops next to me. The window comes down and the guy behind the wheel says, "Don't believe I know you." He doesn't say anything else, just sits there looking at me. Beside me I can feel Frankie getting all tensed up, and I know the last thing I need right now is for her to start barking at this policeman. He looks like he's having a bad day already and wouldn't mind taking it out on somebody.

It pisses me off that he's all but accusing me of something, even though I know that can't be right. I haven't done anything, and all Frankie did was pee, so I didn't even have to think about getting out one of those little plastic bags. I know I need to get out of here before I say something or Frankie does something that gives him a reason to get out of his car.

"No, sir, I don't think you do," I say, trying to settle myself down. "I'm just on my way to Jackson and my dog Frankie here had to pee, so I pulled in here. I figured since it was an empty parking lot it wouldn't be a problem."

He looks down at Frankie, who's not moving a hair, and says, "That your dog?" I nod. "What breed is he?"

"Frankie's a she, sir, and I don't really know. Got her from a friend of mine when she was a pup. Runt of the litter, and he couldn't find anybody that wanted her. She's not a full-blooded anything."

He nods and there's a minute where nothing happens. He's sitting in his car looking out the front windshield, I'm standing there with Frankie, and I don't know if I'm supposed to say something or not.

"Well," he says, still staring straight ahead, "the man that owns this property drove by a little while ago and called us, said there was a truck he didn't recognize in his parking lot, and would we check it out." He looks at me and then at Frankie. "You weren't planning on breaking into his place, were you?"

Now I am really pissed off. I didn't go anywhere near his stupid building. Looks like it wouldn't take much to just knock it down. I'll bet there's nothing in there worth stealing.

"I believe I asked you a question," he says.

I know how you're supposed to talk to cops. We all learned that about the time we got our license if we didn't already know it. I didn't get a license when I was supposed to, but I sure learned how you're supposed to act. Daddy damn near got himself thrown in jail one time when we got pulled over and he started in on the cop who was standing at his window. If Momma hadn't been there to calm him down I don't know what would have happened. You're supposed to say, "yes, sir, no, sir, thank you, sir" and all that shit, make them feel like they're real important. Even then sometimes they don't let you go, but it's what everybody does. So I do that, too.

"Yes, sir, you did, and I only pulled in here to let Frankie out into the grass right back there," I point toward the back of the parking lot, "and I thought we could stretch our legs a little."

The cop doesn't say anything for a second, and then he says, "We're a small town here, son, and we know pretty much everybody. We like it that way. You understand me?"

"Yes, sir, I do. I was just putting Frankie in the truck when you pulled in, and we'll be on our way as soon as I can get her in and get in beside her."

He nods. "That's a good idea. You have a pleasant day now." He rolls his window up but doesn't move, waits until we pull out, and follows us until we've gone about five miles or so. I look in the rear view mirror and see him swing onto the gravel beside the road and turn his cruiser around to head back the way he came.

I'm trying real hard to just keep driving, not too fast, just keep moving. What I want to do is go back and tell that son of a bitch to kiss my ass and Frankie's too, but I'm not sure even Daddy would have done that. Anyway, I know I need to get away from his little town, so that's what me and Frankie are doing.

If this is what Alabama is like, when I get across the state line I'm never coming back, that's for damn sure. I'm hoping Mississippi will be friendlier. I don't guess you can judge a place by its police, but I think if everybody's like that guy, it's a wonder all the kids don't move out as soon as they get old enough.

I know I saw the car turn around, but I keep checking in the mirror for the next fifteen minutes or so, until I finally decide that I'm being stupid. If he'd wanted to do anything he'd have done it already.

When I get into Mississippi I find a place to pull over just outside someplace called Laurel and get Melvin's map out. I'm not good yet at figuring distance from one place to another, but it looks like it's a lot shorter trip to New Orleans than Memphis. Right about now it'd be nice to have one of those GPS things Tiny has on his truck, but probably Melvin made it all over the place with one of these paper maps, and I figure I'm only going to a few places before I head back home. I'm thinking New Orleans should be next, partly because it's closer and partly because both Melvin and that old couple at the RV park said I needed to eat some New Orleans food.

Chapter Eight

The part of Tennessee I'm from has lakes all over the place, but I've never seen anything like this Lake Pontchartrain. It must be twenty-five or thirty miles across the damn thing, plus I have to pay $3.00 just to get on the bridge. I almost tell the guy there was no way in hell I'm paying to drive on a bridge, but when I look in the mirror there's a bunch of cars behind me and no real good way to turn around, so I give him the money and he raises the bar to let me go on across.

That gets me into Metairie, and when I look at Melvin's map it looks like it's right next to New Orleans. He had told me to go to the French Quarter; it's kind of hard to read the streets because of the circle he drew around it. He went round and round a bunch of times, and I can't hardly read some of the street names, but I finally get it figured out and head for the French Quarter.

I don't usually have to think much about where to

park the truck, but the closer I get to Bourbon Street the more crowded it is. By the time I cross Canal Street I'm scared I might not be able to find a spot anywhere. I make a left on Conti Street and after a few blocks there are cars parked on both sides of the street, and there's a couple of open spots. I pick one on my side and pull into it. There's not a lot of room and I spend a lot of time going back and forth until I'm lined up.

When I get out and get Frankie on her leash I notice there's a couple of guys watching us. One of them says, "Guess you failed parallel parking in driver's ed, right?" and both of them start laughing.

The only driver's ed I ever had was Nancy, and that was mostly driving around the back roads and going over that little book so I could pass the written test. I guess parallel parking is what I was supposed to be doing to get the truck into that really tight spot.

I don't say anything to them, and after a second one of them, the short one, says, "You just now get into town?"

Frankie is sitting, just watching what's going on. She's not worried about these two guys so I'm not either. I've gotten to where I depend on her anytime I meet somebody new, which I'm doing a lot of on this trip. Finally I say, "Yeah, just drove in."

The other one doesn't say anything for a minute and then he says, "We're heading over to Bourbon to get some red beans and rice. You hungry?"

I am pretty hungry, and I'm trying to remember whether Melvin said anything about red beans and rice. He talked about New Orleans food like it was the best thing you could put in your mouth and he did say something about rice, I'm pretty sure. It takes me a second to remember.

"Is that like dirty rice? I got a friend that told me if I came here I needed to eat some dirty rice."

"Nah," he says, "we're just talking about regular red beans and rice, but there's a couple of places that really spice it up. It'll set you on fire if you're not used to it," and he grins at me.

Most of the food I ate at home was pretty plain, so I don't know how I feel about spicy stuff. What I had at Jericho's, some of that had a little kick to it, so I guess it'll be all right.

They start down the sidewalk. I look down at Frankie. "You want some red beans and rice, girl?"

We get three bowls at a place that has tables set up outside and the short guy, his name is Artie, tries to order beer for everybody and the waiter just stares at him. He looks over at me after the waiter goes back inside and says, "Worth a try, right?"

I shrug. None of us look like we're anywhere close to twenty-one, so I didn't figure we would get any, especially since we're sitting outside right on the street. Bourbon Street is not full of people like I thought it would be. Melvin talked like it was one big party down here that never stopped. I mean, there's lots more people than I'm used to, but it looks like it would be pretty easy to move around.

We're finishing up our beans and rice and people are walking by, and every now and then somebody will stop and ask me about Frankie. Like, what a pretty dog, is that your dog, stuff like that.

Artie says, "You get that a lot, all that attention to your dog?"

I shrug. "I guess so. People seem to like her, and she doesn't mind much."

He gives the other guy a look real quick, I almost don't catch it and don't really think anything about it, and says, "Let's go, man. You got to see Bourbon Street before it really gets any later. It'll be jam-packed by ten or so."

Artie stands up and says, "We've got this. Our treat since you're new in town." He puts a ten down on the table and says, "Ready?"

They know all the places on Bourbon, which place has the best of which kind of food, and they're telling me all about it and every once in a while we stop so they, mostly Artie, can tell some story about the last time they were there. Usually when we do that one or two people will stop and ask about Frankie, and sometimes they'll want to pet her. I usually don't like that kind of stuff, and tell them she's kind of shy around people she doesn't know. About half the time they'll end up taking her picture and once in a while they'll take mine too. I don't know why they'd want to do that.

There is music everywhere on Bourbon Street. Not the kind of stuff I'm used to, but even I can tell these players know their shit. Half a dozen times we stop and join a crowd of folks that are listening. There's usually an open guitar case or cardboard box or an upside-down hat in front of them and people will go up and toss in a dollar or two. I saw one guy put in a twenty.

It takes us a good half hour to get down one side of Bourbon and we end up in a kind of narrow space between two buildings. I'm facing out, looking around at the street and realize that from where I'm standing I can see seven liquor stores. I've never been in a place like this in my whole life.

"Hey, Artie, you know where I can go to get some of those beignets?"

There's no answer so I turn around and the space is empty. Artie and whatever the other guy's name is are gone. I didn't hear them go and they didn't come by me, so they must have gone out the other end. Frankie is still sitting and I say, "C'mon, girl, let's head back toward the truck."

She doesn't move for a second and then, when I step back out into the street, she pulls against the leash. I turn back toward her and she's trying to get to some trash cans that are setting up next to a door about ten or twelve feet back.

"No, Frankie, there's nothing in there for you. Come on, let's head back."

She keeps pulling and I finally give up and follow her in. She's not interested in the trash can after all. She starts nosing around on the ground beside it and when I look down there's half a dozen wallets in a pile, just tossed up against the wall. Some of them look brand new.

"What the hell?"

I'm about to reach down and pick one up when I hear somebody coming up behind me.

"Well, well, look at this. What have you got there, young man?"

I turn around and there's a policeman standing right behind me. He's got his hand resting on his gun and he's looking at the pile of wallets.

"First thing, is that dog dangerous?"

I look at Frankie. She's sitting right by my left leg and doesn't look dangerous to me at all. I start to make a joke about it and then remember that I'm talking to a cop; a lot of them aren't big on jokes. He looks dead serious and his hand hasn't moved off his gun. Then it does move and he pulls out a little can that was right next to the gun. I'm afraid he's about to give Frankie a shot of pepper spray in the face just in case she's a dangerous animal.

Daddy hated the police. I think he got caught more than a few times driving drunk or at least a little lit up and he never was any good at talking his way out of stuff like that. Plus he got in a few fights, so the cops knew who he was, and I guess once they know who you are you're screwed. Anyhow, he used to tell me, "Those assholes are out to get people like us. If you're rich you get away with all kinds of shit, but not us. Not us." He'd go on like that for a while, especially if he was drunk, until he got tired of bitching about how bad he had it.

Until this trip, Deputy Anderson was the only cop I had much dealings with, and he turned out to be an okay guy. I didn't trust that right at first, because of what Daddy taught me, but after a while the deputy and I got along. Since I started this trip I've been hassled out in the middle of nowhere in Alabama for no reason at all, and now I got this cop getting ready to pepper spray my dog. Probably me too, if I give him any reason. There's a part of me that's thinking maybe Daddy was right about people like us.

Whether he was right or not, I've got to figure out what to do about right now. I try to think of what I can say to keep Frankie and me from getting a face full of that stuff. I know that some of these guys like you to suck up to them, so I try that first.

"No, sir, she's a good dog. She's just sitting right

here. She's fine, really. You don't need to worry, sir."

It pisses me off no end to have to kiss his ass like this, but I'm a long way from home and I know I don't need to get in any trouble.

"Assume the position," he says, real mean like, but he's got the spray back in his belt.

When I don't move right away he says, "Hands against the wall! Feet apart! Don't make me say it twice!" He's almost shouting now, and Frankie is getting tense, I can feel it.

"Yes sir, I'm doing it," I say and look down at Frankie. She's almost trembling she's so worked up, and I know this guy's about to put his hands all over me. Frankie's never seen anything like this before.

I start saying, real low, "It's okay, Frankie, good girl, Frankie, it's okay," over and over again and I try to move kind of slow when I turn to face the building so it doesn't freak her out. I have to lean over the wallets to put my hands on the wall and the cop sees them, and it's like he got reminded of how this all started.

He's checking my pockets and saying, "You want to explain that pile of wallets to me?" and Frankie is still under control but just barely. I get ready to grab her in case she decides to jump him when he steps back. He's got my knife in his hand. I never felt his hand go into my pocket. This guy is smooth, I'll give him that.

"Move to the other side of the alley," he says, and I get out of his way as he bends down and picks up one of the wallets. He opens a flap and reads, then looks over at me.

"You don't look like Lloyd Walters, age 47, from Golden, Colorado," he says. He picks up another one.

"Or Sherry Morgan from New Mexico," he says. He doesn't bother with any more of them.

"You want to tell me about them?"

I'm thinking that if I run across Artie and whoever that other kid was I'm going to kick their asses so hard. I guess I don't answer quick enough because he says, "Okay, let's go. There's some folks that want to talk to you about this."

"Okay, okay, just a minute," I say. "The first time I saw those was when you came up on me. I was going to head back up Bourbon and Frankie pulled me over to them. There's no way I had anything to do with this."

I'm trying to decide whether to tell him about Artie and whoever. The worst thing you can be is a rat, I know that, but I never met these guys before, and it's not like turning in your friends. That look that I barely noticed, back when we were eating, I bet that was them setting me up to keep all these people, Lloyd and Sherry and all the rest of them, busy looking at Frankie and taking her picture while they ripped them off.

He's standing there and I know I need to get out of this or I'll lose Frankie. It's for sure they won't let me keep her with me wherever he wants to take me, and that finishes making up my mind.

I decide I don't owe them a damn thing.

"Sir, I just got into town about two hours ago," I say, and then tell him about meeting up with Artie and the other guy and how I think they used me and Frankie to keep peoples' attention while they stole those wallets from them.

"I was just standing here after we finished walking down Bourbon Street and I was looking at everything, they were behind me, and when I asked about where I could get a beignet they didn't answer. I turned around and they were gone. That's the truth, I swear it."

"What was the name of the other guy?"

"I don't know, they never said, I only met them a little while ago."

He doesn't say anything for a minute and then he says, "A beignet, huh?"

"Yes, sir, my friend Melvin, when he told me to be sure and visit New Orleans, said I had to eat jambalaya and a beignet while I was here."

"This guy Artie, was he shorter than the other one? Brown hair, kind of skinny?"

I nod.

The cop nods too. "Artie and Scott, at least that's

110

what they call themselves. We know about them. You say if I'd gotten here earlier I could have caught them?"

I shrug. "I don't know about that, sir. I guess they went out the back of this alley to get away from me and Frankie, and they would for sure have done that if they saw you coming."

Daddy would kick my ass for real if he saw me sucking up to this cop like I am, but right now I don't even care. I can't lose Frankie.

He takes a picture of the wallets, picks them up and puts them in a bag, turns and says, "Come with me."

"But, sir — "

He's still looking away from me. "Don't make me say it again."

I look down at Frankie and I'm about to start bawling like a little kid right in the middle of the street. I think about taking off, but I'm in a place I've never been before and I probably wouldn't make it a block. So I follow him.

He gets to his cruiser, tosses the bag in, locks the door, and keeps going.

We go about three or four blocks and get to an intersection. He stops and points at the street sign. I look up at it; we're at Bourbon and St. Ann.

"Cafe Du Monde is right down there," he says. "They have several locations now, but that one is the original." He turns to face me. "You don't feel like a bad kid to me, so I guess this is your lucky day. Stay away from Artie and Scott, son. They're bad news."

I try to think of something to say. Until he walked on past his cruiser I figured I was headed for the police station and Frankie was going who knows where. I sure as hell didn't expect him to let me off the hook for the wallet thing, much less take the time to show me how to get to Cafe Du Monde.

He's already turned around and two or three steps back down Bourbon Street when I finally decide I need to say something even if it's stupid.

"Sir, I really appreciate this. Frankie does too. I mean — "

He doesn't turn around or say anything, just throws his hand up and keeps walking. I stand there and watch him leave, feeling like a damn fool for not being able to think of something better to say. I never have been any good at coming up with the right words, and this is no different.

"Frankie," I say, bending down to scratch behind her ears, "we just barely got out of that one. If I see Artie again, I'm going to kick his ass good. Him and that Scott kid just about got us split up." I give her one more scratch and stand up. "Let's head back to the truck, girl. We'll come back down here tomorrow morning and get one of those beignets."

I guess I shouldn't feel too bad about those two

assholes fooling me, since they fooled Frankie too. Can't remember the last time that happened.

We take our time getting back to the truck, watching all the people and listening to music. A lot of the bars have their doors open and you can hear a band playing inside. That plus the musicians out on the street and all the people walking around talking and laughing makes this one noisy place. I don't like it this noisy, I decide, and I'm not sure Frankie likes it either.

The quiet never bothered me much when I was back home. It was lots better than Daddy's yelling and cussing, which he did most of the time when he was in the house. Out in the barn, too, but you couldn't hear him as well. I guess that's one reason I liked the pool so much, back up in the woods where the only noise was the creek water and an animal or a bird now and then. All the time I was going up there nobody ever found it, or me, so it was maybe my best place to be.

One of the things I really liked about Gamaliel was that he didn't feel like you had to talk all the damn time, like a lot of people do. Some days we'd just sit in that back room for an hour or two, sipping shine and enjoying the silence. Every once in a while one of us would say, "You want another one?" but that was about it.

When we did talk, it was easy with him, easier

than anybody else I've ever known, easier than Frankie my brother, easier even than Nancy. Way too many times I'd be talking to her and say something or do something and I could see the hurt in her eyes. Sometimes she looked scared, too, and I hated myself for that. Hated my daddy, too, for teaching me that's how you treat women. Sometimes it'd be days before me and Nancy could get back to being good together.

It was never like that with Gamaliel, never felt like I had to watch what I said or be sorry about some thing I said or question I asked. He was the best, no doubt about it.

Damn, I miss that old man.

We finally make it back to the truck and I give Frankie one more bowl of food and a walk around to give her a chance to pee before we call it a night.

Chapter Nine

I find out when I get back to the Cafe Du Monde that when you order a beignet you don't get one beignet. You get three plus coffee for less than five bucks, and it is the best breakfast I've ever had in my life. Nothing else even close. The coffee is really hot and the beignets have sugar sprinkled over them and they're messy to eat and awful damn good. I'm tempted to get another order and some more coffee, but Frankie is getting restless, so I know we need to get out of there. I remember from eating out with Mark that I'm supposed to leave a tip but I have no idea how much a tip is supposed to be, so I sip my coffee and watch until I see somebody getting ready to leave. The guy pulls out a dollar and looks at his wife. She shakes her head and holds up two fingers, and he pulls out another one and sticks them both under the plate. I figure since there were two of them and one of me that if I leave a dollar it'll be okay.

Frankie and I spend a little time just walking

around. We didn't get around to breakfast until the middle of the morning, so things are opening up in the French Quarter. I don't go into the shops because of Frankie, but I do a lot of looking around, and there's all kinds of shit here I've never seen before. None of it is anything I can afford except the cheap stuff, tee shirts and things like that, and there's places that sell those things, but right next to one of them might be a store that you can just tell by looking has real expensive stuff in it. There are paintings and wood carvings in some of the windows that look like they might cost a thousand dollars, and I see a price tag on one of the paintings that says $1,200.00, so there you go. This is the kind of stuff Raymond and Charlotte would buy, I bet.

I wonder which direction they went when they left the swamp.

It doesn't take long for me and Frankie to get tired of looking at stuff we don't really want and couldn't buy if we did, so we head across Decatur to a big area that has lots of trees. I mean, lots of trees for being in the middle of a city. From what I'm used to, it's not all that many, but I've been looking at buildings and concrete for a while now.

The place is called Jackson Square, and there's a big statue in the middle that I guess is this guy Jackson. It's late morning now, and the place is getting busy, lots of people walking around, and

116

seems like everywhere there are people selling stuff, playing music, dancing, all kinds of stuff going on. Folks sure look like they're having a good time, but for me it's too damn crowded and noisy. Maybe if Melvin was with me and could show me around I'd like it better.

At one edge of Jackson Square there's the biggest church I've ever seen in my life. They don't even call it a church; the sign says it's a cathedral. There are lots of churches at home, little wooden buildings with gravel parking lots, most of them might hold fifty or sixty people. I got no idea how many people would fit into this one. Looks like thousands, maybe.

I'm staring up at the church when somebody says, "That's a beautiful dog you've got there. Is he full-grown?"

"She," I say without looking around. "Frankie's over two years old, so yeah, this is as big as she'll get."

"Ever thought about breeding her?"

I look over to my right where the voice has been coming from and there's a guy standing there. He's not looking at me; he's looking down at Frankie. She mostly ignores him, which I think is a good sign. She was wrong about Artie and Scott, though, so maybe she's getting this guy wrong too.

He's a black guy, maybe a little younger than Mark, I guess, but I'm not any good at that kind of thing. He sticks out his hand and I take it. "Armstrong," he says. "Name is Louis Armstrong."

"Boone," I say, " and this is Frankie."

He looks at me kind of funny and doesn't say anything for a minute, and then he says, "So, no jokes?"

I don't know what he's talking about so I don't say anything. Neither does he, and after a minute I say, "Jokes about what?"

"My name," he says, like that's supposed to clear things up.

I shrug. "I knew some Armstrongs back home. Never had much to do with them. How come you're asking me about breeding Frankie? I had her fixed, so I couldn't even if I wanted to, which I don't."

"So the name Louis Armstrong doesn't mean anything to you?" he says, like he can't believe it.

I shake my head. "Is it supposed to?"

"Never mind," he says.

I go back to looking up at the cathedral and after a minute or so look around and he's still standing next to me.

"Where are you from?" he asks.

I tell him Tennessee. I guess I'm supposed to ask him where he's from, so I do.

"Right here," he says, "I've lived in New Orleans my whole life, except for about a year after Katrina."

I don't say anything. He looks up at the sky and

118

then says, "I was just a kid, maybe about your age." He looks at me and then away. "Maybe older." His head drops and now he's looking at the sidewalk. "Nobody should have to go through that. We all thought we were dead.

"The government, from Washington on down, either didn't know what to do or didn't care. You know how we got out?"

There's no way I could know anything about that, and I'm about to tell him so when he starts talking again.

"A guy came by in a boat. He wasn't a police officer, Army, Coast Guard, anything. Just some guy, got ahold of a boat, and started looking for people. I found out later there were dozens of people like that. No telling how many folks they saved."

I'm thinking about the fire at Tiny's farm, about how people just showed up.

"I get that," I say.

He looks at me like I'm crazy or something. "How could you possibly know about that?"

Now I'm all embarrassed, so I don't say anything else.

Louis shakes his head. "For a while the Mississippi ran backwards, did you know that?"

Now I think he's probably lying. Rivers don't run backwards.

"You don't believe me, do you?" Louis doesn't wait

for me to answer. "You can look it up if you want to. Katrina was so strong it pushed the damn Mississippi River back up toward Baton Rouge." He's looking at the sidewalk again. "One mother of a storm, that was."

"So how come you came back?" I ask him. "I mean, couldn't it happen again, you know, another storm like that?"

"This is home," he says. Then he raises his head and looks me straight in the eye. "This is home," he says again.

He stares at me for a long time and then shakes his head. "Sorry, Boone, sorry. I get started talking about it and it's all right back here in my head. You're probably here for a good time, right?"

I shrug. "A guy I knew told me there were a bunch of places I needed to see while I was young and gave me a map he'd marked half a dozen cities on. New Orleans was one of them. He said the food here was amazing."

Louis takes out his phone. He hits one button and holds it up to his ear, looking at me while he waits on somebody to answer.

"Hey, it's me. What are you cooking tonight? . . . . . Great! Set out an extra bowl, I've got somebody here from out of town who needs to taste the real thing. . . . . Okay, see y'all at seven."

He puts his phone back in his pocket and grins at

me. "You are a lucky guy, Boone. Momma makes the best gumbo in New Orleans, and she's cooking up a big pot tonight. She always makes more than we can eat, so we're good." He puts his hand on his heart. "Tonight you're going to experience New Orleans perfection."

I don't really know what gumbo is, but if you eat it out of a bowl maybe it's some kind of stew or something. Louis is being awful friendly to somebody he just met; I think about it for a minute and decide it must be Frankie, since he asked about her right at first. Probably he figures if I've got a dog I must be okay.

I get that, especially since Frankie isn't one of those mean dogs some people have. Some of those guys strut around with their dog on a chain instead of a regular leash acting like they're ready to pick a fight, them and their dog both. I can't stand folks like that and try to stay as far away from them and their dogs as I can.

The only time Frankie's ever acted like she was ready to fight is when she figured something bad was about to happen to me if she didn't. She keeps me safe as best she can, and I don't know what I'd do without her.

Then I remember something Melvin told me. He said, "If you make it to New Orleans you'll meet the friendliest people on the face of the earth. There's really no other city like it in this country."

So maybe it's not Frankie. But it could be. She's the best dog there is.

Louis is looking at me with a kind of funny expression on his face, and I realize that I haven't answered him at all. Just been standing here like an idiot. I try to think of something to say.

"That sounds really good, Louis, thanks. I have to bring Frankie, I hope that's okay with your family."

He waves a hand at me. "It'll be fine. I didn't tell Momma on purpose. She's going to love Frankie. She's a dog person, been one all her life."

I nod. "So what is gumbo, exactly?"

He laughs out loud. "Just you wait, Boone. It's a little bit of heaven right there in front of you, at least the way Momma makes it."

He tells me to meet him back here at a little after six and then says, "I got to get out of here, late for a meeting, so I'll see you this evening."

Frankie and I spend the day checking out the French Quarter and I'm thinking about how wrong I was back home when I thought it was hot and humid. I remember three or four summers ago I was complaining to somebody, I forget who it was, and they said, "This is nothing. You ought to see what Memphis is like."

It's hard for me to think that Memphis could be worse than this. I'm sweating like I've been hauling hay for hours and all I've done is walk up and down the street. Frankie's panting like crazy, but a couple of the restaurants that have tables outside have bowls of water just sitting there, so Frankie stops at one and almost drinks it dry. Some guy is standing inside the place looking at us through the big window, and when he heads for the door I figure we're in some kind of trouble for drinking his water, but when he gets outside he says, "That's a beautiful animal you have there, young man. What breed is he?"

I explain that Frankie's a she and I don't know what all kinds of dog she is, and he nods and says, "They're smarter and healthier than purebreds, nine times out of ten. Give me a mixed breed dog any day of the week."

He tells me to wait a minute and goes back inside. When he comes out he's got a plastic glass of ice water and a half a sandwich of some kind. He puts them on one of the tables and says, "My staff always makes sandwiches for lunch and I thought I remembered there being a few left over." He points to the table. "Have a seat in the shade and let me know if the sandwich is edible. The new guy made them and I'm still trying him out."

One time Momma brought home a paper bag full of tomatoes from the store. She was telling me and Hannah that the owner had just given them to her because he was going to have to throw them out, they were about to go soft or something like that, and Daddy heard her. He was sitting on the couch and I guess she thought the TV was loud enough for her to talk, but he came in screaming about us not taking charity from anybody and he wouldn't eat those damn tomatoes if he was starving and neither would any of us. Momma tried to keep him from throwing them out into the yard and he reached in the bag and pulled one out, shoved it right into her face. It made an awful mess, and she kind of fell back against the counter. He grabbed the bag and slammed the kitchen door hard on the way out, and I could hear him cussing and the tomatoes going splat against the side of the house.

I'm standing there in the French Quarter in New Orleans and it's all I can do to keep from screaming myself. Daddy just won't get out of my head and I hate him for that. I know how shitty his life was and how he tried to make ours just as bad, I guess so he'd have company, and ever since I got out from under him I've been fighting to keep from going down that same damn road. Here this guy is trying to do something nice for me and I'm about to tell him no or something even worse, and I'll be damned if I do that just because it's what Daddy would have done.

"You all right, son?" I hear the guy say. "You don't look so good."

Frankie bumps my leg and I look down. She's got her eye on that sandwich and I know I'd better do something quick, so I say, "I'm good. Just not used to the heat here."

I sit down and I'm about to say thanks when he reaches into the pocket of the apron he's got on, pulls out a napkin, and unwraps what looks like a little pork chop. "I never could understand why somebody would just walk away and leave a perfectly good pork chop on their plate," he says. "Looks like they only cut off one bite. Okay if your dog Frankie has this? I'd hate to toss it in the trash."

Frankie's sitting still but just barely and her eyes are locked on that piece of meat.

When I don't answer right away he says, "Don't worry, it's not old. I have a customer who comes by once a week or so for an early lunch. Today she brought a friend, and he left this on his plate. Not sure what she sees in him; anybody that would waste food like that, I just do not know."

He sure talks a lot, but that's okay, because it gives me a chance to kind of get over Daddy's voice in my head and remember my manners. Mark told me one time that if somebody offers you a gift, don't try to figure out what's behind it, just say "Thank you."

I nod. "Frankie would love that. Thank you."

I take a bite of the sandwich. "Tell your new guy his sandwich is really good. What do I owe you?"

He looks a little hurt, and I guess I messed up somehow. Maybe Mark was right, and I should have just said "Thank you" and left it alone.

Before I can say anything to try to make things right, he takes a step backward and says, "Nothing, you don't owe me anything. I was going to throw it out anyway." He turns and goes back inside.

I finish the sandwich. Frankie takes about five seconds to eat the pork chop. I sit there for a minute trying to figure out how to fix this and finally give up.

"Come on, Frankie. I've screwed this up and don't know how to make it right, so I guess we ought to get on out of here." I think about leaving a tip and realize that'd be like slapping him in the face, so I don't do that.

He's still inside, but I can see him in there moving around. I get a good hold on Frankie's leash so she doesn't run inside and open the door. "Just wanted to say thanks," I say when he looks over in my direction. I close the door before he can say anything in case what I just did was the wrong thing too, and Frankie and I head on down the street.

The thing about the heat and humidity in this place is I don't have my woods. Course I lost them when I moved into Gamaliel's house, but they were still right there, close by. Now all I've got is concrete and asphalt and what they call parks here that have half a dozen trees and a couple of patches of grass, which compared to the Smoky Mountains shouldn't even be called a park. I'm thinking I'm going to melt right into the sidewalk. Frankie and I go from one shady spot to another and end up back at Jackson Square in the middle of the afternoon.

It's way too early to meet Louis so we go on back to the truck. I figure I ought to change clothes, and Frankie can curl up under the truck for a little while to get out of the sun. I might have to crawl under there with her.

We get back to Jackson Square a little before six, and Louis shows up about a quarter after. "I hope you're hungry," he says when he comes up to us. "Come on. You can ride with me and later on I'll drop you off wherever."

He's parked a couple of streets away and when we get in the car it's probably 20 degrees cooler than outside. I put Frankie in the back seat and drop into the front. Louis climbs in and I say, "This is the coolest I've been all day."

He laughs. "If your car doesn't have air down here, you're in bad shape."

On the way to his house Louis tells me about Katrina.

"We live in Metarie now, but we were in New Orleans when the hurricane hit," he says. "Houses were underwater, people hanging onto the ridges of their roofs, just hoping somebody would come by."

I nod like I understand, but I don't, not really. I try to imagine Gamaliel's house underwater, or the old folk's home, or Nancy's parents' place, and I can't do it.

Louis is still talking. "We were lucky, I guess. We got out of the city, but a lot of people couldn't. Didn't have a car, no relatives to call for help, or if they could call somebody they couldn't get into the city to bring them out. They opened up the Superdome for people to stay, and that was terrible, from what I heard. Not enough of anything, bathrooms, cots, blankets, food. Nobody had expected the levees to fail, so they didn't prep the way they should."

"What's a levee?" I ask.

Louis looks at me like I'm some kind of retarded kid. "You don't know . . . . okay, I guess you don't have any need for levees where you come from. Didn't you study about them in school, though?"

I don't want to tell him I pretty much blew off school about halfway through my sophomore year and didn't go at all the year I was supposed to be a senior. There's a part of me that kinda wishes I hadn't done that, but it's too late to change that now.

He doesn't wait for me to answer, just goes on. Turns out a levee is a big wall, like fifteen or twenty feet high, that keeps the ocean out if it tries to come in. I don't understand that much, either, but about that time we pass a cemetery and I say, "What are all those little buildings?"

I guess Louis has given up being surprised at how ignorant I am. "In lots of places we can't bury our dead in the ground, you just dig a little ways and the grave starts filling up with water. Those are tombs for our relatives after they pass."

I'm starting to understand why Melvin wanted me to do some traveling. This is nothing like home, and I think he wanted me to see how different another place can be from the only place I know. I haven't figured out yet whether this traveling is going to make me want to never go back to Tennessee or get back there as quick as I can.

Louis keeps talking about New Orleans, and Katrina, and a big party they have down here every year in the early spring, Mardi Gras, where people dress up in fancy outfits and wear masks and party for sounds like a week or two. I don't know whether I'd like that or not, especially when he tells me it gets so crowded you can't walk down the street.

His parents' house is nice, a little bigger than Gamaliel's, but not so big you couldn't find your way around. It's all jammed up pretty close to the houses next door, but there's a little bit of a yard I can see on both sides. Can't see the back yard, if there is one. There's half a dozen cars in the driveway and on the street, and Louis says, "Looks like my brothers and my baby sister are here. Come on in and I'll introduce you and Frankie to everybody."

Frankie is a big hit with Louis' mom and the rest of the family, too. He's got two brothers, one older and one younger, and one sister. His older brother is Miles and his younger one is Charlie, and they all think it's hilarious that I don't get it, whatever it is. His sister's name is Billie, which I think is weird for a girl, but maybe not as weird as Jericho, so I guess it's okay.

"Billie's supposed to mean something too, I guess," I say to her. She's sitting on the couch in the front room and Frankie would be in her lap if I'd let her. She's scratching Frankie behind the ear and talking to her real low and stops long enough to give me a funny look, and then she's right back to talking to my dog.

Sometimes I feel like this is Frankie's trip and I'm just along for the ride.

Chapter Ten

The gumbo is really really good. We didn't eat hardly any rice when I was at home, so I don't put much in my bowl, and I fill it up to about halfway with gumbo. Everybody else fills theirs right to the top and they pass around a little bottle of red stuff. They shake some into their gumbo and when it gets to me Louis says, "That's Momma's homemade hot sauce, Boone, and it's powerful stuff. You might want to try just a little bit, at least at first."

"Louis, what's the matter with you?" Miles is sitting across the table from me and picks up the bottle where I'd set it down. "It's not gumbo without Momma's sauce." He puts so much on his gumbo that there's little pools of it on top and then he passes it back to me. "Don't be shy, Boone, you got to put enough on there to taste."

He starts mixing his all together. I look at my bowl and then around the table. Everybody's watching me and I figure the polite thing to do would be to put a little more on there, so I do. I set the bottle down and mix mine up like Miles did.

When I'm finished I look up and everybody's still watching me. "Go on," says Miles, and he's got a look in his eye I've seen before. I'm pretty sure this is going to set me on fire, but I'm in too far to back out now. I'm about to take a bite when Charlie says, "Where is Boone's beer? Did y'all expect him to eat gumbo without a beer next to him?"

He opens a bottle and sets it down next to my bowl and says, "Now you're ready."

I figure I'd better not wait any longer or I'll chicken out, so I take a good-sized spoonful and put it in my mouth. At first I just taste the gumbo but after about fifteen seconds the heat starts and I feel like my insides are melting. I put the spoon down and pick up the beer, take a drink, and say, "That's pretty good." I take another bite and it's still fiery, but I'm getting used to it. I look over at Miles and say, "Can I have that bottle back? I might need just a touch more."

Miles starts laughing so loud it fills the room and scares Frankie until she realizes what it is. Billie's laughing now, too, and everybody else, and even their momma's got a little smile on her face. I turn to her and say, "Ma'am, this is awful good. I appreciate you making room at your table for me and Frankie."

I don't know anything about cooking, but it tastes

so good I figure she must have spent a lot of time on it. I start to ask her about that, but before I can she says, "Boone, I'd sure like to meet your mother. She certainly raised you right." She looks around the table. "You boys see that? Nice and polite, even after you tried to set him on fire, Miles," and she shakes her finger at him.

The rest of the meal is great, lots of talking and joking around and eating gumbo. I catch Billie looking at me once or twice with a kind of funny look on her face that I can't figure out. Once when I catch her eye she looks right at me for a good two seconds, smiling a smile you can barely see. I don't know what to think about that, but then she turns and says something to one of her brothers sitting across from her and I go back to the gumbo. Frankie gets a few pieces of whatever kind of sausage this is from a couple of people; I think Charlie gives her more than anybody else. He's kind of sneaky about it, so I think that means it's against the house rules.

Toward the end of the meal we're sitting around the table, just taking it easy, when Billie says, "So, Boone, you surprise me a little. Here you are sharing food with us at our table, looking all comfortable, and I bet you have never even had a meal in a black family's home before. I mean, do you even know any black people back in Tennessee? Now, before you say anything, Momma," she holds her hand up, "I know

Boone is a guest in your home and we're supposed to be polite and all, but you know everybody here is curious about that. I just thought I'd go ahead and say it, get it out in the open." She looks me right in the eye. "Well?"

All during the meal I've been thinking about Mark. He's really the only black person I've ever known besides just to say hi and stuff like that. Mark isn't like Louis' family; he's got a lot of preacher in him even though mostly he acts like a regular person. I spent a lot of time with him and he helped me through a bunch of shit, didn't preach at me unless he just couldn't help himself, plus I saw how people treated him just because he was black and it make me think about how people looked down on me without even bothering to get to know me. I said that to him once; he said it wasn't the same thing at all and I believed him, but still it made me think he ought to have been treated better.

When I look up from my bowl everybody is looking at me.

I clear my throat and say, "Well, there was this guy named Mark . . . ."

I tell them about the first time I met him and how he talked me into saying all that stuff about Gamaliel, about what the old man meant to me, and how he helped me through half a dozen hard times of one kind or another.

"I mean, it really didn't bother me that he was black," I say, and that really sets things off.

All of a sudden the whole table is talking all at once and somebody, I'm not sure who, says, "Well that's mighty big of him not to be bothered" and somebody else, or maybe the same one, says, "Typical white man's talk, always up above us in their own minds" and somebody else is saying that as far as they could tell I wasn't holding myself above anybody, and somebody says, "Like we need his permission to be okay" and it's pretty clear that what I said was wrong but I'm not sure what was so wrong about it.

Then Mrs. Armstrong says real soft, "Everybody hush now," and the place goes dead quiet, just like that.

"First of all," she says in that same soft voice, "do not talk about our guest as if he wasn't sitting right here with us. Second, do not talk that way about anyone we invite to a meal at our house whether they are in the room or not. Do I make myself understood?"

Nobody says a word, but everybody nods and Louis looks like he's just gotten a whipping. Charlie looks like he nodded just because his momma told him to, not because he believes it. Billie is staring into her bowl like there's something real interesting in there, and Miles has his head down and his arms

135

folded and I can't tell anything about what he's thinking.

If I had my truck here I'd just get in it and go. It's real uncomfortable right now and I'm afraid somebody's going to start throwing things or swinging fists any minute. That's what would happen at my house, except Daddy usually didn't let anybody but him talk, and the throwing and swinging only started when one of us crossed him or he thought we did.

Frankie has been glued to my leg ever since things got loud. Before she was settled in one corner after making the rounds at the table, but now she's right next to me, leaning in and real tense. I can feel it. She's not growling or anything like that, but she is on edge. So am I, as far as that goes, but since I rode over here with Louis, I can't really go anywhere.

She turns to me then. "Boone, I'd like to apologize on behalf of my family. Sometimes they forget their manners."

I know I need to say something here, but damned if I know what it is. Mark would know, Nancy would probably know, but I sure don't. I sit there for a few seconds trying to think of what to say that won't start things up all over again.

Finally I clear my throat and say, "Ma'am, I figure I said something that kicked this whole thing off. Not real sure what it was, but I didn't say anything out of meanness. If I said the wrong thing I'm sorry about that." I stop and look around the table and see that they're all looking at me, and I say the only other thing I can think of. "Don't guess there's any more of that gumbo, is there?"

Billie stares right at me for a long second, and then her mouth twitches a little bit. Then she starts laughing out loud, and after she catches her breath she says, "It's almost gone, Boone, but you can have some if you want it. If you don't save room for dessert, though, you'll be sorry. I can promise you that."

"Tell the truth, I hadn't even thought about dessert," I say. "Maybe I'll wait for that. Your gumbo was awful good, ma'am," I turn to Mrs. Armstrong, "but if there's more food coming I better take a pass on another bowl full."

Frankie's still right beside me, but she's not as tense as she was before. She always has been better than me at figuring out if there's something wrong. If she's feeling better maybe it's going to be okay.

Then Miles pushes his chair back and it makes an awful noise on the wood floor. He stands up and looks around, everywhere but at me. He says, "I'm going to be skipping dessert tonight. Momma, your gumbo was as good as always. I'll see you all pretty soon." He's halfway to the door before Mrs. Armstrong says anything.

Actually she starts to say something and Charlie waves at her from the other end of the long table. "It's okay, Momma, I got this."

He gets up and moves across the room. He opens the door and shouts, "Hey, Miles, hold up a minute." The door closes and he's gone. Everybody else just sits there for a minute or two.

Frankie hasn't moved from right next to me, and I'm thinking about what an old man, his name was Mr. Rankin, told me one day when we were out in the yard at the old folks' home sitting in the sun. Frankie was curled up on the ground between us, and he reached down once in a while and scratched her behind one ear.

"You know, if you're the kind that wants to, you can fool a lot of people in this world." He looked down at Frankie. "You can't fool dogs, though." He sat there for a second. "Or children. Dogs and children. They know if you're a good guy or not."

Right now I'm sitting in a room with a bunch of people I just met a couple of hours ago, in a strange city, miles away from my truck, and I'm not real worried, and I realize it's because Frankie's not worried. Miles was pretty upset, I think, but nobody at the table seems to think anything bad is about to happen.

One thing about this trip is, I'm starting to figure out just how screwed up my family was. If this kind of thing had happened at home, we'd all be scared shitless for at least the rest of the night and maybe into the next day, wondering what Daddy might do.

That's a pretty damn stupid way to live.

"Boone, honey, are you all right? You don't need to worry about Miles, he just gets that way sometimes. Half an hour and he'll probably be back wanting some of that dessert he turned down just now."

Mrs. Armstrong is looking at me with a kind of a worried frown on her face and I guess I've been sitting there staring at the wall for a while.

I like Mrs. Armstrong and she's been real nice to me, but there's no way I'm going to tell her I've been thinking about what an asshole my Daddy was.

"Sorry, ma'am. I'm fine, thanks for asking."

I don't say anything else and it's kind of uncomfortable for a few seconds and then Louis says, "Well, Miles might be willing to skip dessert, but I'm not. What are we having tonight, Momma?" and everybody relaxes a little bit.

Mrs. Armstrong acts like it's no big deal but when she says one of her pecan pies is about ready to come out of the oven and there's vanilla ice cream to go with it, Billie raises her hands up toward the ceiling and says, "Praise be, I've died and gone straight to heaven!" She looks over at me. "If all this is because you're here, Boone, you just keep right on coming by around dinner time. Every other day at least, all right?" She smiles at me, mostly with her eyes, and gives me a wink.

I grin at her and say, "I'll have to check with Frankie and see if it's okay with her, but that sounds pretty good to me."

The pie is awful good, maybe the best pecan pie I've ever had, and hot out of the oven with a big scoop of vanilla ice cream on top, well, it's damn near perfect.

Nobody talks for about five minutes. Not a word. All you can hear is forks scraping until all that's left is a little ice cream, and then everybody switches to spoons. About that time the door opens and everybody turns to see who it is.

Charlie comes in first, with Miles a couple of steps behind him.

Chapter Eleven

Miles walks straight over to his momma and sits down. She glances at him and then looks away. He's real quiet, and so is everybody else, and after a few seconds she turns back to him and he says, "I'm sorry, Momma, for being rude and disrespecting our home that way."

She shakes her head. "I'm not the person you need to apologize to," she says and tilts her head in my direction. "You take care of that and then come back and talk to me."

I can see him tense up.

Frankie feels it too, and goes from lying down at my feet to sitting with her head right next to my left hand. She's not doing anything, just sitting there, but I can tell she knows something's not right.

Nothing happens for what seems like a long time. Everybody is waiting on Miles to do whatever it is he's going to do. Even though everybody's on edge right now, this doesn't feel like it did back home with

Daddy because here things were so good just a little while ago. With Daddy good times were few and far between, so we always had our guard up, ready for things to go wrong. My brother Frankie would miss the early signs sometimes and so he'd be the one who set Daddy off, but if it hadn't been him it would have been one or the other of us. Evenings pretty much all ended up the same way. It's almost worse here because of how much fun we were having before I opened my big mouth about Mark. I'm the reason things are so tense here, and I know it. I figure everybody else does, too, and I'd get out if I could, but I'm stuck here waiting for what I'm afraid is going to be a bad end to what was a really good dinner.

Then Billie says, "I don't think there's anybody parked behind me, and I have some stuff I need to take care of at home." She turns toward me. "If you're staying in the city somewhere I can give you and Frankie a ride back unless," and she gives me a wink, "you're planning on some more of that pie."

She stands up and before her mother can say anything, Billie says, "I know, Momma, I know we're not supposed to run right out of here after we eat, but some of us have jobs to get to tomorrow, so I really do have to go." She looks over at me. "Well, Boone, you and Frankie need a ride?"

I don't know whether she's doing this to get me out of this or herself out of it, but I'm glad to have the chance to get back to the truck. I nod and look over at Mrs. Armstrong, "Ma'am, that was a fine meal and maybe the best pie I've ever had in my life. I appreciate you letting me join you." I look around the room. "Real nice to meet all of you."

Miles looks like he's about to say something, but he shakes his head instead and then looks right past me to the door like he's telling me to get on out of here.

I think that's a great idea.

Frankie and I follow Billie out to her car. It's a little thing, might fit in the bed of the pickup, and there's only the front seats, but there's room for Frankie to squeeze in behind them. We get her settled in and head toward the city.

It reminds me of riding in Mark's Mini, and I watch Billie work through the gears. She's as smooth as Mark was, and it makes me think of the first time I tried to drive his car there in the parking lot. Billie looks over at me and says, "What are you smiling about, Boone? Thinking about your girlfriend back home?"

I shake my head. "My friend Mark, the guy I told you about at dinner, has a straight shift and I was thinking about the first time he let me drive it. I was awful."

She's quiet for a minute. "Miles is who taught me." After another half a minute or so she says,

"Listen, about back there . . . ."

I don't say anything.

Billie clears her throat. "He's not usually like that, Boone, he's a good guy. Maybe something happened at work today, I don't know. I just thought it'd be a good idea for you to leave before he said something that would get him in real trouble with Momma."

I nod. "I appreciate the ride. I was feeling a little stuck, not having my truck there and no way to get back to it. Didn't think about that when I told Louis yes to the dinner invite. Course I didn't know then how far away Mrs. Armstrong's house was from the city."

I'm just rattling on, and Billie's got a little smile on her face like she knows a secret of some kind. I finally run out of stuff to say and we ride along without either one of us saying anything, and I'm looking out at the sky going dark and over at her and around at the traffic and back to her and pretty soon I'm just staring at her.

She's really good looking, I decide, although I don't have a lot of other black girls to compare her to. There was a guy at the home, used to add half and half to his coffee a little at a time and stir it. Then he'd look at it and pour in a little more. Over and over again until he was satisfied. He told me it had to be just the right color. His coffee looked like caramel when he got done. Billie's that same shade of brown.

144

She's got a dress on and it's all bunched up about halfway up her thighs. I guess she must have come straight from work to her momma's house, since she and Louis were the only ones there that were dressed up. She catches me looking and I turn away but I hear her laugh kind of low and when I turn back she's grinning at me.

"I'm a little curious myself, but you and I both know there's no way I'm taking you home with me, Boone," she says. We're at a traffic light, right behind an old minivan with Arkansas license plates and a bumper sticker that's too old and faded to read. I nod and don't say anything because I can't think of anything to say that wouldn't be stupid as hell, so I just sit there.

Billie's looking at the van now. "If I did and Miles found out about it, well, I don't know what he'd do to you. I know I'd hear about it every time I saw him from now until Christmas after next. That guy can say some really mean things." She turns back to me. "You understand?"

I nod again. I can feel myself hard as a rock and I'm glad it's getting kind of dark because I know I'm blushing like crazy. All I can think of is, here's this really good looking woman talking to me like we're both used to doing it and we just can't decide whether to do it with each other or not.

The light must have changed. The car behind us

honks four or five times and Billie holds up her middle finger, but the guy probably can't see it because Frankie's in the way. The minivan is way ahead of us by now and Billie puts the accelerator on the floor and we jump ahead so fast I'm slammed back against the seat.

She catches up to it in a heartbeat and slows back down. I can hear Frankie scrambling around in the space behind the seats trying to get comfortable again after being thrown around.

Billie's not looking at me now. She's paying attention to the traffic. It's getting more crowded and she has to get more serious about driving. She glances in her side mirror and then back to straight ahead and says, "Besides, every other woman you'd have for the rest of your life would be a big letdown."

I look over at her and she looks dead serious, but then her mouth twitches a little bit like it did back at the house, and then she's laughing big and loud and I can't help it, I start laughing, too.

Finally I say, "Well, I might be willing to take my chances on that," and we start laughing all over again and I think we're going to have to pull over so we don't end up in some kind of accident with that Arkansas minivan.

Billie is the first girl I've felt this easy around since Nancy, and I don't know what to think about that. I mean, I know it isn't right that I'm feeling this way about a black girl, but I don't know exactly why it isn't right. Daddy would say it's wrong, and so would Momma, I'm sure about that. Actually Daddy would do more than say something. He would beat my ass if he thought I was even thinking about doing anything with a black girl. Tiny and the rest of the people my age at home would probably tell me it's not right, too. I remember that waitress when Mark and I had lunch together and how she treated him, like he wasn't even a person and she was just waiting on me. I'm pretty sure I know how she would feel. And Nancy, well, it might be more personal with her, but I bet I know what she would say about the way I'm feeling right now.

When I get to Gamaliel I realize that I have no idea how he felt about black people. It just never came up all those times we were talking, and when I try to figure it out I get nowhere. I know he never called them niggers like Daddy did, and never talked about them like they were less than anybody else. It's hard to say that, really, since he never talked about them at all. Like he never talked about Mexicans, or women, or preachers, or anybody. I know he didn't like rich people, called them filthy bloodsuckers that lived off the work of honest men and never turned a hand themselves, but that's the only group of people he ever ran down in all those times we talked. I always figured he'd gotten screwed over by some rich guy and carried that with him, couldn't let go of it. Everybody else, though, he didn't have anything bad to say about them.

Well, there were those two guys that tried to rob him, that time that I got shot trying to help him out, but that wasn't really a whole group of people. It was only those two, and it was just because they were coming after him and his stuff. They didn't know about the money he had stashed in that little box, of course. At least I don't think they did. I found out about it when he was in the hospital and I was looking after his place, but I don't see how they could have known. Probably they were just thinking an old man would be an easy target. Turned out they were wrong about that. And there was Jerry. Gamaliel didn't have much use for him, and I know I didn't.

But that's a pretty short list, a lot shorter than most other people probably have. As far as I know, the people Gamaliel didn't like were people he could call by name. I don't think Gamaliel gave much thought to big groups of people. Probably he was too old to worry about that kind of shit.

There's not a whole lot of folks that I know who would be fine with what I'm thinking about right now, and most of them I've met in this last week. Jericho would be okay with it, I'm pretty sure, and Raymond, Denise, and Jeremy. Abigail I don't know about, but I think she would be too.

I'm so wrapped up in thinking about it that I don't notice where we are until Billie pulls the car into a parking space on a street I don't recognize.

"I don't know where you're staying, but Bourbon Street is two blocks that way," she points back over her shoulder.

When I get out of the car and lean the seat forward so Frankie can get out, she stays right where she is. Her leash is in my back pocket and I reach for it, but when Frankie sees it she scoots back farther away from me.

"Looks like she wants to come home with me," Billie says with a grin.

I nod. "I think you're right."

Neither one of us says anything for a second and then Billie says, "Oh, the hell with Miles. Get in the car, Boone," and she pushes the seat back into its place. I hear it click, and at first I just stand there outside her car, but it doesn't take me more than a few seconds to decide what to do. I get back in and slam the door shut. Billie looks over at me and grins.

"Fasten your seat belt, Boone. It's going to be a bumpy night," she says. I fumble around for a second and get buckled up. When I look over at her she's shaking her head at me. Then she backs up a little to get some room and does a u-turn in the street, makes a right at the next intersection, and floors it.

Chapter Twelve

I wake up to what sounds like rain, but it isn't, exactly. When I'm in the back of the truck and rain is hitting that metal roof right over my head, it's a great sound to go to sleep to, but this isn't loud enough. Frankie isn't next to me, which isn't right either. For a second I'm panicking, thinking I've gotten separated from my dog somehow, and then I hear her. She's close by, but I don't see her anywhere. I sit up and look around, trying to figure out what's going on.

The rain noise stops and I realize it was a shower in the next room. I'm in a bed, a real bed, and it's a mess. The sheets are tangled up all around me and it takes me a minute to get loose.

While I'm getting untangled Billie comes through the door. She's got a big towel folded up in one hand and another one just like it wrapped around her waist. "Shower's yours, Boone, but make it quick. I have to get out of here soon if I'm going to get to work on time."

She tosses me the folded towel. She unwraps the other one and starts drying her legs. I can't take my eyes off of her; she's so beautiful, like nothing I've ever seen before. Her hair is tucked up inside of some kind of cap. She takes it off and shakes out her hair, then looks over at me. "I said make it quick. If I'm going to give you a ride back to your truck you have to leave when I do." She grins at me. "If you're hoping for more of what we did last night, you're out of luck. I've barely got time for breakfast." She looks straight into my eyes. "Although calling in late is sounding pretty good right about now." Then she laughs that big laugh of hers and says, "If you want breakfast here you better get your ass out of my bed and into the shower."

I get to my feet and unfold the towel. I start to hold it in front of me and then think, that's stupid, and throw it over my shoulder instead. When I'm about to go through the bathroom door Billie says, "Soap and shampoo are already in the shower. Don't use any of my products. They're not for your kind of hair."

Product is some kind of special stuff for black people's hair, I guess. Most of the time at home we just had soap and used that for everything, but when I look in the shower I see eight or ten bottles, most of them stuff I've never heard of. There's a bar of some kind of fancy soap, with colors all mixing up and what looks like flower petals inside it. I find a tall bottle that says "Jasmine Shampoo" on the little shelf, so I don't pay any more attention to the rest of the bottles.

I make it quick so Billie won't be late for work. When I come back out into the bedroom Frankie is sitting on my pants looking at me like, "Can we go back to the truck now?"

"We'll be heading out soon, girl, I promise," I say, and give her a scratch behind the ear. Then I pull my pants out from under her and put them on.

Frankie looks at me like she's not sure she believes me. I head out of the bedroom door and follow the noise to the right. There's a big room that's a kitchen at one end and a living room at the other, with a little table in between. Billie is dressed for work already, sitting at the table with a cup of coffee and a plate in front of her.

"I don't know what you Tennessee boys eat for breakfast, but here you've got bagels and cream cheese and some cantaloupe. Coffee to drink. You want your bagel toasted?"

She can tell by the look on my face that I don't have the slightest idea what she's talking about. "I swear, Boone, you need to get out more," she says. "Of course, I guess that's what this trip is all about, right? Here, let me do it for you," and she is up and at the counter before I can say anything. She slices the bagel and sticks it in a toaster. The thing looks like a donut, but when I get it out and put it on a plate it's hard on the outside and chewy on the inside and not sweet at all. I try the cream cheese and decide it's pretty good, and I know about cantaloupe already, so I sit down opposite her and say, "This is real good. I appreciate it."

She raises her cup to me and I do the same thing, and I start eating. She's about half done already, I can see, and I don't want her to be late on my account, so the only time I take a break is to give Frankie a little bit of bagel.

"I don't have any dog food for you, girl. Sorry about that," Billie says. "You want some of my bagel, too?" Frankie trots over and sits about as close to her chair as she can get and Billie laughs. "So that's a yes, right?" she says and tears off a piece.

She leans back and looks over at me, studying me before she says anything. "You know, if you'd told me early on it was your first time I would have gone easier on you." She smiles. "Although you kept up just fine and figured things out right away. I mean, it didn't even bother me that you're white."

I'm thinking, who the hell is she to be saying that kind of shit about me, when I look over at her and see a little grin on her face. Then I remember my comment about Mark last night that set Miles and

154

everybody else off and damn near ruined the dinner, and I have to smile back at her.

"Gotcha," she says.

I dip my head a little bit. I'm not sure what to say right now, but after a second I decide I might as well just tell her what I'm really thinking. "To tell you the truth, Billie, I didn't have any idea it could be that good."

"I told you last night in the car, Boone, every other woman from here on out is going to be a big letdown." She looks like she's about to start laughing, but instead she gets quiet for a minute and then says, real soft like she's talking to herself, "When it's done right it's about the best thing there is."

I nod.

"And we sure did it right," she says, and stands up. "Finish that last bite of breakfast. I've got to be out of here in ten minutes, fifteen at the most." She takes a long drink of coffee.

Her cell phone plays a little bit of a song and she answers it. She gets up and starts walking around the living room and I can hear her part of the conversation. Sounds like work, something about a meeting that was supposed to happen this morning getting canceled. She sounds mad when she's talking to whoever it is, but when she hangs up she looks over at me with a big smile.

"Guess we're not in such a hurry after all," she

says. Then she comes back over and sits down. "Not enough time to head back in there," and she tilts her head toward the hallway, "but we can take our time, have another cup of coffee, and you can tell me about Tennessee. I've never been anywhere east of here. All my trips have been Texas, Colorado, places out west. So tell me about where you come from."

I try to think of something good to tell her about. She knows about Mark and some about Gamaliel, and I don't want to talk about my family. Right then, while she's making another pot of coffee, she says over her shoulder, "You have family back there in Tennessee?"

There's no way she could know what I'm thinking about. I feel like I have to get her onto something else, so I say "Not really," and start right in talking about the woods behind the house, how in the early morning there's sometimes fog that looks like it's weaving in and out of the trees, and how the creek sounds in the summer when everything is green and all the leaves soften the sound a little.

The pool where I used to go when things were really bad with Daddy had different light patterns depending on when you were there and what season it was. In the spring the skaters would dart around on top of the water and every once in a while a fish would rise up and try for one. In the summer the woods were so thick that you were completely cut off from everything outside and it took a real loud noise to get through.

I'm going on about the woods and the trail to Gamaliel's house and finding the still and fighting the fire up at Tiny's place when Billie sets a fresh cup in front of me. I skip the part about Jerry and tell her about running the ridges with Frankie and what it looks like in the mountains when the colors peak and finally stop to take a sip of coffee.

The coffee's still in my mouth when I remember Abigail and what she said about Benton's bacon being better than sex, and I barely get it down before I start laughing. I manage to set the cup down without spilling any of it, take a deep breath, and I can't help it, I start laughing all over again. Billie's looking at me like I'm crazy and I hold up my hand while I try to get myself under control.

"There was somebody back in Tennessee, about a week ago, bought me a biscuit with Benton's bacon and told me that some people said it was better than sex. I didn't want her to know I was, you know, so I didn't say anything. Of course now I know that's bullshit. Nothing could be better than last night." I grin up at Billie, who's leaning against the kitchen counter. She doesn't grin back, just shakes her head and starts to say something and stops. She takes another sip instead.

Then she says, "One of the fanciest restaurants in

New Orleans, the kind where you have to make reservations three months out, says they only use Benton's bacon. They make a big deal out of it. How do you know about Benton's?"

I shrug. "Abigail said that Mr. Benton's farm was just up the road from where we were, not real far from where I grew up, so I guess your fancy restaurant gets their bacon from Tennessee."

"Well, I'll be damned," Billie says. She smiles at me. "Well, anyway, good to know I'm better than Benton's."

"I guarantee it," I say. "Cross my heart."

I take another drink of coffee. It's still hot. "I gotta say, I'm a little worried now. You reckon you really did ruin me for anybody else?"

"Well, if I did, I don't want you to come whining back to me about it. You were warned." She tries a serious look that lasts about ten seconds.

It's still real easy with Billie, and I was afraid after last night it wouldn't be. I really didn't know what I was doing, so I figured I'd be doing it wrong at least some of the time. If I was, she's not holding it against me, so that's good.

Come to think about it, there's a lot of stuff I don't know how to do. Never was a big deal back home, everybody was pretty much alike except the rich folks and I never had anything to do with them. It's sure different out here.

158

I didn't know how to get the shell off the shrimp at the beach, or even what some of that other food was. Or what to do about drinking wine with a steak dinner. Me and Gamaliel, the only reason we ate anything while we were drinking shine was because that stuff would've put us on the floor or sent us into the back yard to throw up if we hadn't. I didn't know enough to figure out that Artie and Scott were using me to rip off those people on Bourbon Street, or how to thank that restaurant owner without pissing him off. Hell, I didn't even know how to read a damn road map.

And I sure didn't know anything about sex.

"Stupid," I say real low, but not low enough.

"What was that?" Billie says.

"Nothing," I say, but it's too late.

"Not nothing," she says. "You said stupid. Who are you calling stupid?" She's looking at me like she's got a pretty good idea of who I'm talking about.

"Me," I say. I'm not looking at her. Frankie comes over and sits right next to me.

Billie goes back to her chair and puts down her coffee but doesn't sit down right away. She stares at me hard for a second and then says, "Because you got it on with a black girl? Is that it?" She sounds mad, or something, I'm not sure what.

Man, I did not see that coming at all. I look up at her and I think she can tell by the look on my face

159

that I'm not talking about that. I shake my head no, and start talking and it all comes pouring out, all the stuff I was just saying to myself I end up saying to her.

When I stop for breath I keep my eyes on the table where they've been the whole time.

"Boone," she says, real soft.

I look up and she's got a little smile on her face but she's mostly real serious.

"You're not stupid, Boone, you're ignorant."

She holds up her hand before I can even get started. She can see how mad I am at her for calling me ignorant.

"My daddy told me a long time ago that an ignorant person is someone who hasn't learned yet, and a stupid person is someone who can't learn. You are not stupid. You proved that last night, remember? We both know you can learn." She smiles. "With the right teacher, that is."

She reaches over and puts her hand on mine. "I'll tell you what I think, Boone. I think the old man who told you to go on this trip did you a huge favor. If you had stayed where you were you could never have learned all the things you're going to learn now that you're out on the road. Plus," and she leans back in her chair and opens her arms wide, "you would never have met me."

I have to smile at that.

"Well," I say. "You do make good coffee."

Billie wags her finger at me. "You watch how you speak to me, Boone. I just gave you the best introduction to the pleasures of the flesh that you could have possibly gotten. Show a little respect."

She gets up from the table. "I need to get to the office by ten and it's," she looks into the kitchen, "a little past nine-twenty. Can you be ready to get out of here in fifteen?"

"I'm ready now," I say. "If you've got some more stuff to do maybe I ought to take Frankie outside for a walk. She's been inside for a while now and probably needs to pee."

She nods. "I'll come find you when I'm ready."

I tell her to drop me on Bourbon close to the Cafe du Monde, and it turns out to be only about ten minutes away. When we get there she pulls into an open spot and leans over. "You take care, Boone, and make sure you look after this excellent dog." I lean in to meet her and our goodbye kiss is almost enough to make me change my mind about leaving New Orleans.

She pushes me back. "I need to get out of here, and so do you," she says. "It was a real pleasure to meet you and," she winks, "get to know you so well." I get out and pull the seat forward. This time Frankie gets out without any problem and Billie says, "Goodbye Frankie, you beautiful girl. Take care of

Boone for me, okay?"

I start to say something else and can't think of anything to say, so I close the door, she pulls out into traffic, and just like that, she's gone.

When we get back to the truck I open the tailgate and get out Frankie's food dish. Those four or five pieces of bagel were just enough to make her hungry, and she finishes off the food in about ten seconds.

"Let's walk around a little, girl," I say, and we head off, away from Bourbon Street, and spend ten or twenty minutes stretching our legs.

Most of that time I'm thinking about last night.

"I wonder if she really did ruin me for anybody else," I say, half to Frankie and half to myself. I'm thinking about whether or not it might have been worth it and thinking probably it was when Frankie gives a short bark and I snap out of it in time to keep from running into a guy with a cup of coffee in one hand and a newspaper in the other. He's not watching where he's going either, and we are just about to crash when Frankie stops me.

I step sideways real quick and he doesn't even see me. He's talking to himself and I hear him say, "What the hell were they thinking?" but then he's halfway down the block.

"Wonder what he's all worked up about?" I look down at Frankie. "Thanks, girl. I just about ran right into him."

162

I'm not paying attention either, though, to tell the truth. Last night was so good I can't stop thinking about it. Billie's apartment was dark when we got there and stayed that way, mostly, because she grabbed my hand and led me straight through to her bedroom. I remember her saying, "Sorry, Frankie, this is private," and rubbing her on the head before closing the door.

The bathroom light was on, and she turned on the two lamps beside the bed, but there was plenty of shadow, and Billie moved in and out of the light, dropping clothes on the floor, quiet until she said, "What are you waiting for, Boone?" and she was standing there naked with the light shining in from the bathroom and I couldn't say anything. All I could do was stare, until I finally kicked off my shoes and got out of my clothes. I climbed into bed with her, wondering what the hell I was supposed to do next.

Frankie barks again and I look up to see a man with his back to me waiting for the light to change so he can cross the street. I'm about two steps from running right into him.

"I got to snap out of this, girl," I say to Frankie, but I know that's not going to happen anytime soon. I'm thinking I need to find a bench and just sit for a while instead of walking around running into people. I was going to hit the road for Memphis this morning, at least I thought about it a little bit, but right now

163

I'd cause a wreck or run somebody over for sure.

There's nothing around me but buildings so we turn around and make our way back to the truck. I put the tailgate down and get Frankie a drink. That bagel is about gone and I'm going to need some food myself before long, but I think for right now I'll just sit.

I try closing my eyes, and I'm right back in the bedroom last night, and it's scary and fantastic all at the same time. Billie was good to me, I gotta say that. She showed me what to do and let me know when I was doing it right, sometimes just with little noises I could barely hear. We did stuff I've seen on movies and some other stuff I'd never heard of or even thought about. I found out a lot about what girls like and what they don't, and some stuff about me that I didn't know that I'd like, but I sure did.

I'd love to go back to Billie's place now that I know what I'm doing, sorta, but I don't know exactly where that is. Plus she's at work, and I don't know where that is either. Or where her momma lives, or Louis. It'd be nice to see her again and do all those things we did last night one more time before I leave town. I'm pretty sure that's not happening, though.

"I sure wish I could run into her again, Frankie," I say, and she looks up from her empty dish like she's ready to do something besides just sit here and listen to me feeling sorry for myself.

164

Chapter Thirteen

We take one more walk down Bourbon Street and end up back at Cafe du Monde. I get half a dozen beignets for the road and a cup of their coffee.

"Let's get Melvin's map out and figure out how to get to Memphis," I say to Frankie, and we head back to the truck. Melvin had said something about Beale Street, so I guess we're going there. I hope it's easier to get to than Bourbon was.

When I look at the map there's an interstate that runs from New Orleans up to Memphis, and it looks like it's about 400 miles. I'm trying to find a way to get there that keeps me off the interstate when I start thinking about Billie again. Not about the sex this time, though. About some of the stuff she told me.

I take a deep breath and take a sip of the coffee and try to think about anything besides Billie. I'm not having any luck, and I'm about to give up and just start driving when somebody says, "Are you lost, young man?"

I look up from the map and there's a couple of old people standing on the sidewalk next to the truck. Frankie's looking at them but she must not be worried about them, since she didn't even tell me they were there.

They're not old, I guess, not really. The woman, the one who asked me if I was lost, looks a little like Betty, the woman who runs the home where Melvin lives, and Betty's not old like Melvin and the others. Maybe the same age as Momma, but I don't know. I think sometimes Momma just looked old because she was so sad.

"No, ma'am, not really. Well, maybe. I'm trying to get to Memphis and I'm not sure which way is the best."

She turns to the man. "Reeves, why don't you see if you can help? You're better at directions than I am."

I don't know what the hell kind of name Reeves is, but I've run into some weird ones on this trip already and this is just one more. If he can help me out here I'll be glad, though, since I'm not getting anywhere. All I'm doing is staring at the map and thinking about last night.

Reeves sits down next to me on the tailgate and says, "So, Memphis. You have family there?"

Here we go again.

166

I start to tell him it's none of his damn business why I want to go there. People that don't even know me keep on asking me all kinds of personal shit. I'm tired of it.

It takes me a second to get past that. I know I'm looking at this Reeves guy like he's out to get me some way, and I know just where that's coming from. Who knows how long it's going to take me to let go of Daddy's bullshit; it sure seems like it's always there. This Reeves guy, he's just doing me a favor. It's stupid for me to get all bent out of shape about that.

Reeves says, "So, no family in Memphis, I assume. You have business there?"

"Hush, Reeves," his wife, at least I guess she's his wife, says. "You can be awfully nosy sometimes. Can't you help the boy out without all those questions?"

She looks over at me, then down at the ground and shakes her head. When she looks back at Reeves she says, "I mean, can you help this young man and his beautiful dog get headed toward Memphis?" She smiles at Frankie.

Reeves is acting like he doesn't hear her. He's looking at the map and kind of talking to himself, and then he looks up at me. "Are you in a hurry to get there?"

I shake my head.

"Well, then, I would stay off the interstate. It's a boring drive, in my opinion." He looks back down at

167

the map.

After another minute he says, "Okay. What I would do if I were starting from right here is," he looks at the street signs on the corner, "make a left up there and another left to get you headed back that way," he points. "When you get to Decatur make a right and just keep going until you get to the Causeway. You need to pay a toll to get over Lake Pontchartrain."

"I know, that's how I came in."

He nods. "It's the easiest way out of here. When you get across stay on 25 until you get into Mississippi; you'll have a lot of choices after that. Highway 61 runs close to the river and would take you all the way to Memphis. That would be a pretty drive, but you'd have to work your way over to it."

The idea of figuring out how to get from one place to another from Melvin's map doesn't scare me anymore. A week ago it would have, but not now. I'm getting plenty of practice.

I nod. "Thanks, I'll do that."

Reeves says, "You have a good trip now. Hope you enjoyed our fair city."

Old man, you have no idea how much I enjoyed my time here.

The old couple move on and I remember to say thanks but I'm almost too late. They're halfway down the sidewalk. Reeves hears me, though, and gives me

168

a wave. He doesn't turn around and neither does she.

"Come on, Frankie, before I forget how to get out of here," I say, and we get into the truck. I make the turns and get onto the road that heads toward the big lake, and I'm back to thinking about Billie and what happened just before we went to sleep.

It was all about her dad.

She really wanted to talk about him last night, I guess. She told me that they lost him in Katrina. He wasn't a healthy man, diabetes and probably a lot of other stuff, and it was just too much for him. He was funny and smart and maybe the best dad anybody could have, she said. She laughed when she told me how he named his kids.

Her whole name is Billie Holiday Armstrong, after Billie Holiday, the singer. She said that her brother Miles is Miles Davis Armstrong, and Charlie is Charlie Parker Armstrong. Louis is the only one with a normal middle name, she said, since Louis Armstrong Armstrong would be too weird, so Louis got Daniel for a middle name.

She said her daddy used to use the four of them as a test whenever a new person moved into the neighborhood. He'd show the guy a family picture and tell him his kids' names, and if the guy didn't get it, her daddy would figure he wasn't worth getting to know any better. She said they got a reputation for being kind of snobby because of that. He wouldn't stop, though. He told her it was an easy way to weed out the ones he wouldn't have anything in common with anyway. I thought that made pretty good sense, and told her so.

I also told her I wouldn't have passed her daddy's test, since I'd never heard of any of those people. She knew that, she said, but it didn't really matter since he was gone. She got quiet after that and I just laid there next to her not knowing what to say or do. Finally I reached out and rested my hand on her stomach. She turned toward me and scooted over until she was curled up against me. That's how we went to sleep. The next thing I knew I was waking up all by myself in the bed trying to figure out where I was.

Getting out of Louisiana is pretty easy with the directions Reeves gave me, and it's a good thing, too, since I keep thinking about last night. I make it into Mississippi before lunch and look for a place to pull over and study the map. Reeves had said something about 61, so I'm thinking maybe I'll see what roads will take me over to it.

It doesn't take much studying to figure out how to get to 61. The south part of Mississippi is pretty empty. There's a Highway 98 that heads over to someplace called Natchez and I'm real close to it already. I get on 98 and just before I hit Natchez there's 61 heading off to my right.

There's a lot of little towns the first part of the trip, until I get through Vicksburg. Then we start driving through a bunch of farms and stuff and it's way different than what I'm used to.

Flat. I've never seen anything like this, much less driven through it. Going down to Caswell Beach and driving through south Alabama on the way to New Orleans was flat compared to what I'm used to, but here the road just stretches out in front of me, no hills or dips or curves or anything. Some of the fields on both sides of the road are completely empty, but some of them, more the farther away from Vicksburg I get, are covered with plants that have white stuff all over them. I finally realize it's cotton when I see a sign over a turnoff that says somebody's cotton farm. The fields are huge, bigger than anything we have up in Tennessee. I try to imagine hauling hay out of a field that big and I get tired all over just thinking about it.

It's real easy to stop paying attention on this road, and that just about gets me and Frankie in a wreck. Some old farmer on a tractor pulls out onto the road ahead of us, and I'm on his ass before I know it. He's doing about fifteen, like all those guys back home, but back there the hills and curves keep us paying attention, and if we're in farm country we know to watch for guys pulling balers or rakes or whatever, especially this time of year. On this road I can't get a

171

good feel for how far away things are. I get the truck slowed down enough to keep from plowing right into him, and he's only on the road for a little bit before he pulls off into a field, but it was way too close for me. For the next ten or twenty miles I'm all tensed up, but after a little while I settle back down to driving and ten minutes later I almost run through a stop sign. I don't think I like driving in Mississippi much.

It does give me some time to think about stuff, though. According to the map, now that I'm on 61 it's a straight shot to Memphis, and it's not like there's a lot of hills and blind curves like back home. So as long as I don't run off the road or rear-end a tractor, the driving part is easy.

I'm still thinking about Billie, but not just about how great the sex was. I wonder what kind of job she's got. One she gets all dressed up for, I know that much. And Louis has a job, too. Raymond had one, but I guess now he doesn't have to work so he just farts around in that big RV. I have no idea if Jericho and that crew had jobs and were on vacation or if they were a bunch of rich kids that didn't have to work.

We've got some folks back home who don't work, but not because they're rich like Raymond. The ones I know that don't work are drawing a check from the government. Some of them need it, I know. Mr. Willington, I can't think of his first name right now,

172

has been in that wheelchair as long as I remember. They say he was working on a car at Dale's Auto Repair and a jack slipped. And Mrs. Michaels, all she does is take care of her son. He can't hardly even make a whole sentence or get himself dressed. She gets a check for him, I guess, and maybe for herself too. I don't know about that. Plus all the old folks who got too old to work, they get a check, but I reckon they earned it.

And then there's the Arlingtons. I went to school with their middle boy, Jackson, and me and everybody else stayed away from him. Mean as a snake, and I heard the whole family was. None of them ever turned a hand at anything, but they all got a check. Jackson showed up one time with a brand new pair of work boots that he said he got because his mom had just got paid. He thought that government check was a paycheck, and he'd be getting one as soon as he turned eighteen. We all knew those boots weren't ever going to see any work. He'd more likely use them to stomp somebody's ass. Closest any of them ever came to working was going out and spotlighting a couple of deer when they wanted some fresh meat. Nobody messed with any of the Arlingtons. They were bad news, every one of them. Even Deputy Anderson didn't mess with them unless he had to.

Nobody thought that family was worth a damn, I

know that for sure. The whole town looked down on them, even Daddy. "Worthless," he'd say. "I wouldn't piss on one of them if they were on fire." My Daddy was a real asshole to me and Momma and Hannah, and sometimes even Frankie, but he was not a lazy man. I got to give him that. He always had work of some kind, even if it was a shitty job. If we passed one of the Arlingtons or drove by their house, he'd say something about there being some people who just wouldn't pull their own damn weight.

Pretty much everybody looked down on us, or at least on Daddy because of his drinking and how he'd pick a fight with just about anybody, so I guess him finding somebody to look down on was just the way things worked. Probably the Arlingtons looked down on all of us for thinking we were better than them.

This kind of shit makes my head hurt. I don't really care about who looks down on who except when it happens to me, so I don't know why I got started on this. Probably because there's not much to see out here but fields, and I've seen a lot of those already.

I don't like having to think about jobs but that money Gamaliel left for me is going to run out sooner or later, and I'll have to do something. I know everybody I went to school with is either working or in some kind of college or trade school. School's out, since I never bothered to finish high school, so I guess it's going to be a job for me.

174

All my jobs so far have been summer stuff, like hauling hay whenever they needed an extra hand. That thing at the old folks home, I think that was more charity than a real job. Probably Carrie and Brenda made that up when Jerry was about ready to kick me out of Gamaliel's place. Never did seem like real work, and it didn't take long for me to start remembering what Daddy used to say about taking handouts from people.

"So, what do you think, Frankie?" I look over at her. "You think I ought to think about getting a real job when we get back home?"

She's ignoring me, like she does sometimes.

Find something useful to do. That's what Raymond had said just before he pulled out of the campsite in Georgia in that big RV. I guess that's kind of what he did when he was working for that trucking company. I couldn't ever do anything like that, though. That takes somebody a lot smarter than me. I don't know how to do anything, really, except make shine and work on farms and stuff. If I was telling the truth I'd have to say that the shine me and Tiny made was pretty awful compared to Gamaliel's stuff. Course he'd been doing it for a long time.

It doesn't matter, anyway. I don't have any of the parts of the still we moved up to the woods on Tiny's farm after Gamaliel went into the hospital. It all burned up in that big fire that Jerry started. Plus I don't have a place to set it up if I did have it all back. And even if I did, with my luck Deputy Anderson would walk up on me before a week had gone by and that'd be the end of that.

What I probably need to do is sit down when I get back home, see how much money I've got left, and try to figure out how long that'll last me. I know I'll end up doing some kind of shitty job if I wait until I run out of money before I start looking around.

There's another tractor up ahead, but I can see for a long ways down the road and there's nothing coming the other way. I slow down a little bit and moved over into the other lane so I can pass him.

After I get past him and pull back into our lane I look in my rearview mirror and he's waving at me. I stick my hand out of the window and wave back. When I look again I can barely see him but it looks like he's still waving. Guess he doesn't see many people out here.

About ten minutes later I see lights flashing in my mirror and think, dammit, I bet I'm speeding. It's so hard to tell on these roads without any curves or hills to slow you down. Turns out it's an ambulance. It goes by me like I'm standing still and in no time it's gone.

I look over at Frankie. "Shit, Frankie, you reckon that guy was trying to wave me down? Like he was in trouble or something?" I spend the next ten miles or so feeling bad about that until I get to the next little town and start having to pay more attention to what I'm doing.

After I get through the town I'm back on this long straight boring road, and back to thinking about what I'm going to do when I get back home, which I'm still thinking is East Tennessee. To be honest, I haven't seen any place so far that I want to stay in for very long. The only place that feels right is where I grew up. I wouldn't even know how to start being anywhere else.

Maybe Memphis will be different.

Chapter Fourteen

Before I get into Memphis, while I'm still in Mississippi, we drive through a little town called Tunica and not long after that I start seeing signs for someplace called Horseshoe Tunica. The signs are all about places to stay and play poker. Everything's off to the left and I don't bother checking it out because I figure there's no place that's going to let me bring Frankie in with me. Besides, I remember Gamaliel telling me once about when he was young, how he got started playing poker with a bunch of guys and realized after a while that he was just giving them a lot more spending money and using up all of the extra money he had, so he quit.

"Don't do that kind of shit unless you've got money you don't care anything about keeping," he had said. "Either you're really good at that kind of thing or you're just giving your money away."

I know I don't have any money to give away, and I also know I'm not any good at gambling. I don't even know how, so I keep driving.

As we get closer to Memphis we go past a lot of big buildings that look like nobody's been in them for years. The glass is broken, there's no lights on or cars in the parking lots, except for a couple of old wrecks that don't even have wheels on them any more. I see a couple of guys hanging out and even from out on the road they look pretty rough, like it would be a big mistake to mess with them. I don't even think about stopping, just keep heading up 61.

Somewhere after we get into Tennessee it stops being 61 and starts being Third Street. It's been a while since I had anything to eat, so I start looking. Melvin had told me that if I made it to Memphis that I needed to do two things. I had to go to Beale Street and I had to eat barbecue.

I go through this big intersection and just past that on the left is a place called Interstate Bar B Que. It's got a big parking lot that's about three quarters full. I don't see a drive-through from the road but I pull in anyway.

When I get to the back of the building there's a guy out there smoking a cigarette. He's got an apron on and he's leaning against the side of the building, watching me drive by.

I stop the truck and get out, get Frankie on her leash, and head over toward him. When he sees Frankie he straightens up and takes a couple of steps toward the door.

"That dog bite?" He looks like he's ready to slip inside and slam the door behind him.

I shake my head. "Frankie's a good dog. Long as nobody's trying to bother me she's okay."

I can't tell whether he believes me or not. "What do you want?"

"I just drove up from New Orleans. A friend of mine told me that if I got to Memphis I needed to eat some barbecue. I saw the sign and pulled in here."

He nods. "Your friend's right. So what are you doing back here? The entrance is around front."

"I don't think they'll let me take Frankie in there, and I can't leave her out in the truck. I was looking for a drive-through or something like that and I saw you here."

He flips his cigarette out into the lot and wipes his hands on the apron. It's covered in big red stains.

"Well, you're at the best barbecue place in Memphis, which makes it the best in the country." He grins at me. "Give me a twenty and I'll bring you out a plate that you'll be telling your grandchildren about when you're an old man."

Twenty seems like an awful lot for a meal and I'm about to tell him to forget it. Then I remember that I didn't really spend hardly anything in New Orleans. Between Mrs. Armstrong's gumbo and Billie's breakfast, pretty much the only thing I bought were those beignets. I pull out my money and look at what I've got. I haven't spent much so far on this trip, so I've still got plenty and that's not counting the money I got from Raymond. I'm trying not to touch that in case something happens to the truck. I hand him a twenty and say, "You keep whatever change there is from that."

He nods again. This guy does that a lot, like that guy back in North Carolina did.

"Be right back."

When he comes back a few minutes later he has a plate in each hand and they're both heaping full. Frankie's got her eye on the food but she's leaving the guy alone, at least for now.

"It's about time for my break so I brought my food out here," he says. "Hope you don't mind."

I shake my head.

"Good," he says. "What's your dog's name?"

"Frankie."

"Okay, don't let Frankie steal my food. I'll be right back."

He's back in a minute with two big plastic cups. He hands me one and holds the other one up. "Here's to barbecue," he says.

I raise mine too and we both take a drink.

"Dig in," he says. "It's better hot." He picks up a rib and tears a bite off with his teeth. "Wish I could have brought out a couple of beers instead of this sweet tea, but I'd get my ass fired. I'm still on the clock."

"That's fine," I say. I look at my plate. There's at least a half dozen ribs, and a big handful of onion rings, and peach cobbler. I pick up an onion ring and dip it in the glob of ketchup beside the pile. It's okay, but the ones at home are just as good.

The ribs, though, are great. The first one, I barely get it to my mouth because the meat is falling off the bone and back onto the plate. The guy hands me a paper towel and says, "I brought plenty of these. Ribs are sloppy eating if you do it right."

I set one rib aside for Frankie, but it's not easy; I could eat twice as much as he brought out. She's waiting over by the side of the truck and I get out her food dish, put some dog food in it. I tear the meat off the rib, pull it apart into little shreds, and mix it in. She's on it like she hasn't eaten in a week, and in half a minute it's all gone. I toss her the bone and she settles down next to the rear tire. He stops eating long enough to point at her.

"What kind of dog is she?"

I tell him she's a mutt, that this guy I knew was giving puppies away because they weren't pure and he couldn't sell them. Frankie was the only one he had left, and she was about to go in the river. She was the runt and nobody wanted her.

"Doesn't look much like a runt to me," he says. He

183

wipes his hand on the apron again and sticks it out. "Erasmus. But everybody calls me Razz."

"Boone," I say and shake his hand.

I've never heard of a name like Razz, and that reminds me of Billie's dad and how he named his kids after jazz musicians. I'm thinking that black people do a lot of weird stuff naming their kids and then I remember that I was named after my parents' favorite wine. I really got no room to talk about weird names.

Razz seems okay. A little nervous, looking around all the time, but he's pretty funny. Lots of stories about working in a restaurant kitchen and how crazy it is. Frankie is kind of staying away from him, though, which makes me wonder a little. In just a few minutes the ribs and rings are gone, and I'm about halfway through the peach cobbler when a woman sticks her head out the back door and looks around. When she sees us she steps over the rock that Razz had been using to prop the door open and heads toward us.

"What are you doing out here, Razz?"

She stops when she sees Frankie and asks me the same question Razz did. "That dog bite?"

I shake my head and finish swallowing the bite of peach cobbler I just put in my mouth. "Not unless she thinks somebody's bothering me."

She looks like she doesn't believe me, but comes

184

on over anyway. She stays on the other side of me and Razz from where Frankie is still working on the rib bone.

"Your break's up in about five and I wanted to let you know Darlene's real mad about something and she's taking it out on anybody that gets in her way. You don't want to be late getting back in there. Not today."

Razz turns to me. "Darlene runs things in the evenings. Usually she's cool but when something gets her going, best thing to do is keep your head down and don't do anything that attracts her attention." I look over at the woman and she's nodding her head.

He looks at her. "What is it this time, Jewel?"

Jewel shrugs. "Who the hell knows? Pretty sure it's nothing any of us did, but you know that doesn't matter." She tilts her head toward me. "So who's this? Friend of yours?"

Razz looks toward me but not right at me. "Yeah. Me and Boone go way back, but I haven't seen him in a long time. He just stopped by and I had a break coming. We're about finished here."

I nod. "Those were some fine ribs, and that cobbler wasn't bad either." He's looking everywhere but at me now. I figure I need to get on out of here, so I say, "Time to go, Frankie." I untie the leash from the truck and take her up to the passenger door.

When I come back around I can hear them

185

talking, but it's too low for me to figure out what they're saying. Jewel steps away and heads for the door, then turns back. "I'm telling you, Razz, you better get back in here. Darlene . . . ." She steps over the rock and slips back inside, still talking.

I don't even want to know what that was all about, and looks like Razz doesn't want to tell me. He says, "I got to get back inside, Boone. Where you staying?"

I point at the truck. "Wherever I find a place to park this thing."

He nods. "Drop back by around 11. We'll get a couple of beers and you can tell me about New Orleans. Never been that far south."

He heads toward the door and pushes the rock out of the way with his foot. He turns and says, "I'll tell you where to park that truck, too. If you want to get some sleep you need to pick the right spot." He waves his hand and goes inside.

I climb into the truck and look over at Frankie. "I don't know about this guy, Frankie. What do you think?" She's still looking at the back door. I don't think she likes Razz, but she didn't growl at him or anything, so I'm not real sure. I'm thinking I might want to pick out my own spot to park for the night.

I've still got a couple of hours to kill before he gets off shift. I start the truck and then shut it off again. I keep thinking about that meeting in Mark's office, when Aunt Claire was trying to get me to go to Memphis to look for Momma. She'd brought Hannah with her to the meeting. That was the first time I'd seen Hannah since I put her on the bus to school that day, and I haven't seen her since.

So not all that long ago Momma was here in Memphis with that son of a bitch Jake, the guy she helped to steal my old truck. He had to leave it on the side of the road because it was such a piece of shit, so that didn't work out too well. I don't know how long they were here, and the last time I heard from Aunt Claire she said that Momma and Jake were moving out west, so even if she was here she's not any more. Who knows where she is.

I try to think about what she was like before Frankie died, and I can barely remember. Seems like she was always scared of Daddy, though, and that makes me wonder why she got married in the first place. I try to remember if there was any time we were happy and finally think of one.

That was the time we moved into the house we were still living in when it all went to hell, when Frankie was still alive. Hannah hadn't been born yet, so it was four of us. We'd been living in a single-wide on somebody's property, I have no idea who, somebody that Daddy was working for. Then he got on with Mr. Wilcox. When he came home and told us he had a new job we didn't think much about it, until he said that there was a house that Wilcox said we could live in if we'd fix it up.

Getting out of that trailer and into a house, a real house, was about the best thing I remember about being a kid. Me and Frankie still had to share a room after Hannah came along, but it was twice as big as what we had in the trailer, so even though we complained about it we didn't mind too much. The bathroom was big, the kitchen was a room all by itself, and we could all be in the living room without sitting on top of each other. There was a yard, and a barn, and woods out back with a creek.

As soon as I start thinking about the barn all the good memories disappear. All I can think about is Frankie getting hurt and Momma and Daddy fighting about the doctor, and then finding Daddy out there after he did himself with the shotgun. I look over at Frankie.

"Let's find a place for you to pee, okay?"

I get Frankie out and look around. There's a little spot of grass next to the parking lot, so I take her over there.

While she's looking for the right spot I'm thinking about what Raymond had said, about me finding something useful to do.

I think that's the way rich people talk. All I'm trying to do is figure out some way to make enough money to get a place to stay and some food for me and

Frankie. I don't much care whether or not it's useful, whatever the hell that means.

When I think about it I realize there's not a lot I know how to do, really, and I'm not interested in going back home and doing whatever farm work there is. Besides, before long it'll be cold weather, so there won't even be much of that kind of job to get. I need to find some other kind of work to do. Maybe I'll ask Razz what it's like working in a restaurant.

Frankie gets finished and we're headed back to the truck when the back door opens and Razz runs out with some woman two steps behind him. She's waving a clipboard and looks really pissed.

"You get back here and look at this!" She waves the clipboard at him. "According to this the men's room hasn't been cleaned in two days! I said get back here!"

He's running toward the truck and pointing at me and at the driver's side door. Frankie and I get there a step before him. We're in when he opens the passenger door and slides in beside Frankie. He slams the door and says, "We better get the hell out of here, Boone, she's coming fast."

I start the truck and turn the wheel hard. She's still coming but I can see she won't make it in time to stop us. I pull away fast enough that she can't keep up but not so fast I throw Frankie around.

Razz points to the street. "Take a left when you

get up there."

Then we're out on the street. Razz takes a deep breath and looks over Frankie at me. He looks back at the street and starts laughing.

"That was Darlene," he says. He starts to say something else and starts laughing. Then he says, "Did you see the look on her face when you left her in the parking lot? Standing there with that damn clipboard in her hand?"

The light up ahead turns yellow and then red after what seems like no time at all. I stop behind a white SUV that looks like it's just come out of the car wash.

Razz points at the SUV. "Hey, that's my man Diablo!" Next thing I know he's opening the door, and I grab Frankie's collar to make sure she stays in the car. "Stay cool, Boone."

He slams the truck door, runs up the right side of the SUV, yanks open the door, and jumps in. The light changes and he's gone.

I look over at Frankie. "Well, I guess he's not going to help us figure out where to park this thing." The guy in the car behind us leans on his horn and I pull out across the intersection without knowing exactly where I'm headed.

Chapter Fifteen

We go a block or two and I pull into an empty lot next to a big building with a bunch of broken windows and nobody else in the lot. I turn off the engine and look over at Frankie.

"So now what, girl?"

Frankie doesn't answer. She's looking out in front of the truck and the hairs on the back of her neck are standing up a little. I look where she's looking and see three guys standing close together about halfway down the block on the sidewalk. They're not coming toward us or even looking at us, so I'm not sure why Frankie is all tensed up. Two of them are black, but I know from New Orleans that black people don't bother Frankie like they do some dogs. A friend of mine back home had a pit bull that would go ape shit if he saw a black guy, or anybody with a hoodie pulled over their head whether they were black or not. Come to think about it, he wasn't real friendly toward anybody, so maybe it wasn't just black people.

Matt said even he couldn't pat the dog on the head or he'd likely get bit. Not sure if the dog was born that way or raised that way, but Matt had his hands full every time the dog was off its chain in Matt's front yard.

Anyway, it's a good thing that black people don't bother Frankie, because that's all there is in this part of Memphis. I never had thought too much about it before, but when I was growing up everybody looked a lot like me. Once in a while we'd get a black kid or a Mexican in school, but except for that we were all pretty much alike.

It looks like it's the same around here, except that pretty much everybody is black, and then there's me. Some of the people going in and out at the restaurant were white, but that's about it. I never thought about what those kids at my school were seeing every day.

I'm kind of half watching these guys and one of them points toward the truck and it looks like they're getting ready to head this way. I'm not real worried, there's only three of them and I've got Frankie with me, but I put the truck in drive and pull out of the lot. No sense in sitting around waiting for trouble when I can see it heading towards me.

Now I'm back out on the street and heading away from the restaurant and further into Memphis, at least I guess that's where I'm going.

I stay on Third Street for a while and turn left,

and in a couple of blocks I come up on Main Street. I turn right so I'm still going in the same direction and head further into Memphis. At first it's a lot like Third Street.

Then it starts getting busier and busier; some of the buildings are all lit up and there's people walking up and down the sidewalk. A lot of the side streets still look dark, and I turn down one. There are cars parked on both sides of the street and on my right is a big building without any windows. There's an open spot about halfway down and I pull just past it and back in. I still suck at this kind of parking where there's barely enough room to squeeze in, but I'm a little better than I was a couple of weeks ago. I get out and look, and I'm pretty much in line with the other cars so I decide it's good enough.

I get Frankie on a leash and we walk back out to Main Street. First thing I notice is I'm the only one with a dog, and everybody's looking at me. Or at Frankie, I guess. Some people have a kind of worried look on their faces; Frankie is kind of big, so I'm not surprised. She's just looking around, though, not really worried about anybody as far as I can tell. One couple walk towards us and the guy says, "Is your dog friendly?"

I look down at Frankie and she's not tensed up, just kind of interested, so I say yeah.

"Can I pet him?"

"Frankie's a girl," I say, and look down at her. Something tells me I need to say no, so I say, "She doesn't like people touching her, so probably not." I see the girl take a step back. "Don't worry, she's a good dog, just doesn't like to be touched if she doesn't know you already."

She's pulling on the guy's jacket. "Come on, Bo, they're waiting on us." She gives me a mean look. "You shouldn't take a dog like that out in public."

Now Frankie's tensing up. I can feel it. I just got to Memphis and already I've been in the middle of whatever was going on between Razz and Darlene, and now I'm getting yelled at for just being on the street with my dog.

I'm trying to keep from saying out loud what I'm thinking when she lets go of the jacket and says, "Fine, stay here if you want to." She starts to go past us and then backs up. She's afraid to go past Frankie.

I tighten up the leash. "Go on by. I've got her." What I'm thinking is that I ought to head back to the truck right now and get out of here. Melvin told me I should eat barbecue and see Beale Street if I got to Memphis. Well, I've had the barbecue and it was pretty damn good, but I don't know whether I'm up for another place like Bourbon Street or not. There's way too much shit going on in cities, and I'm getting tired of it. Always having to worry about people, and not enough room to move around when Frankie's

194

with me, which is all the time.

She keeps as far away from us as she can and still keep on the sidewalk.

When she's past us she looks at the guy. "Well?"

"Be there in a minute," he says.

She just stands there.

"You go ahead," Bo points down the street. "The club is right there. I'll catch up."

I'm not looking at her. I'm looking at him and wondering what is going on here. I guess she must have gone on, because he stops looking over my shoulder and looks right at me.

"Sorry about that, man. Jeannie can be a real bitch sometimes."

I shrug. It's not like I've never been treated like that before.

We stand there and look at each other. Frankie isn't tense anymore, she's just sitting about as close to me as she can get.

Bo looks down at her. "She's a good looking dog. Where'd you get her?"

I go through the story about her being the runt of the litter and about to go in the river when I got her.

"She's not purebred or anything, so with her being the runt and all nobody wanted her."

He nods. "She turned out to be a real beauty. Do the two of you live close by?" and he waves his hand around.

I shake my head. "No. We're out traveling. A friend of mine told me I should see Memphis."

"Mud Island," Bo says after a second.

"What's that?"

"While you're here you should see Mud Island," he says. "There's a park there and you can walk right along the Mississippi."

I nod, but I don't know about trying to find this place just so I can walk along the river.

He points to Frankie. "A lot of places aren't going to let you in if you have a dog, unless it's a service animal." He stops and looks at me.

"What I mean is, you could go to a place like Mud Island and get out, stretch your legs, lots of people there have dogs with them. Long as she's on a leash and you pick up after her, nobody's going to mind you being there."

I shrug. "My friend didn't say anything about Mud Island, just went on and on about Beale Street."

"You're not too far from Beale right now," Bo points up the street. "Of course you can't go in anywhere with Frankie." He stops for a second. "Not that there'd be room anyway. That's why Jeannie and I come down here. Beale's just full of tourists and everybody's jammed up against each other and the music's so loud you can't hear yourself think." He looks at me. "No offense."

I don't even know what that means. It sounds like

maybe I'm going to skip Beale Street.

Pretty much every place I've been on this trip I've run into the same thing. Having Frankie with me meant there were some beaches I couldn't even go to. Most of the Okeefenokee had a no dog rule, and in New Orleans I mostly just walked up and down Bourbon Street. Bourbon had those places to eat outside, so that helped some, but still. I guess lots of places don't care much about people with dogs, or most people who have dogs leave them somewhere when they go out to eat or whatever.

I haven't even thought about leaving Frankie in the truck since Abigail almost took out my side window with a hammer. Even if I was willing to, I sure wouldn't leave her there in a strange city. No telling what might happen to her.

"You okay, man?"

Bo is still standing there. Frankie's sitting right up next to me like she does sometimes, leaning against my leg.

"Yeah, I'm fine."

"Okay. Well, I'd better catch up with Jeannie," he says. "Nice to meet you." He kind of acts like he wants to shake my hand but then he just steps around us and walks away.

I don't even turn around to watch him go. I'm looking at the sidewalk full of people and all I can think about is getting out of here. Maybe I'll feel different after a night's sleep.

"Come on, Frankie. Let's go back to the truck. Maybe we're far enough away from all this noise to get some sleep."

It takes a little while for things to quiet down enough for us to go to sleep, but we finally do. The next morning there's a bunch of banging outside the truck and when I get up to see what's going on there's a couple of guys collecting trash.

I get Frankie's dishes out and feed her. The jug I use to fill up her water dish is almost empty, and I give her what's in it. It's not much.

There's got to be a place around here I can refill this, but I don't even know where to start looking.

One of the trash guys is watching me. He says something to the other guy and walks over to us.

"Nice dog," he says. "You live around here?"

I don't know why everybody asks me that, but I guess we do the same thing back home. I shake my head.

"Looks like you need some water for her," he says. He holds out his hand. "Give me that jug."

I hand it to him and he runs back to the truck. It's stopped at a red light and he opens the door on the passenger side and reaches in. He comes out with a big water cooler and sets the empty milk jug on the sidewalk. Frankie and I start walking toward him and by the time we get there he's just about finished filling up the jug. "There you are," he says, and takes off after the truck. It's about half a block away from him, but he catches it the next time it stops.

I don't even get a chance to say thanks.

The truck turns the next corner and he gives us a wave, and then he's gone.

"Well, at least now we don't have to try to find you any water for a while," I say to Frankie. "Let's see what this place is like in the daytime."

Beale Street doesn't look like much where it crosses Main Street. I turn right and there's an open parking space on our side of the street, so I pull in there. Frankie and I get out and head away from the river and by the next block there's bars and restaurants on both sides of the street and even though it's morning you can hear music coming from a couple of places.

There's a guy, maybe about my age, standing in the street. I'm still a little ways off from him when he starts running. I can't figure out what he's trying to run away from when he starts doing flips, going from his hands to his feet, over and over. He does about a dozen and ends up next to two other guys. They look like they're about the same age as him. The three of them are laughing and joking around, and the guy that just finished his run bows to the other two.

Then one of them, the taller one, starts running right toward us. He's still 50 yards away when he starts that same kind of flipping. He's coming really fast, and Frankie starts growling a little.

"It's okay, girl," I say, but I understand what's going on with her. She's never seen anything like this before. I think it's kind of neat but it's sort of freaking her out.

He pulls up short of us and gives us the same kind of bow the other guy did. He starts to walk over to us and Frankie stands up. That stops him ten feet away or so, and he says, "That dog cool?"

I look down and Frankie doesn't look freaked out anymore now that the guy's not doing all that crazy shit. She's still standing up but I can tell she's not worried about him, so I say, "Yeah, she's cool."

He takes a couple more steps and stops. "You sure about that?"

I nod.

"Okay," he says, and comes up close enough to stretch out his hand. He lets her sniff the back of it and waits until she starts wagging her tail. "What's her name?"

"Frankie."

He straightens up then and says, "What kind is she? I've got a couple dogs at home. Got mine from a guy I know, he wasn't sure what breed they were. They're sisters, is all I know."

Seems like I'm telling this story a lot, but I go through it again, about my friend whose dog had pups that weren't pure anything so they were just giving them away. How Frankie was the only one left, the runt, and was about to go in the river when I got her.

He shakes his head. "Man, good that you came along. Be a shame if they just threw her away like that."

I look down at Frankie. "Yeah, it would. She's a pretty good dog."

I don't tell him she's pretty much all I've got.

"So how come y'all are running up and down the street like that?"

He gives me a look. "You're new in town."

"Yeah, got here last night."

"Well," he says, "starting about three in the afternoon this place is going to get busy, people all over the streets, and they'll all have money. We put on a show and they put cash in the can." He grins. "It's an easy gig. We come out early in the day so we can practice. Nobody's going to pay to see us fall on our ass, right?"

He points to the other two guys. "Now, I'm the best, but Junior there is pretty good, and Luke is, well, he's just getting started. He needs this morning stuff more than we do, but we all come out here so we can stay sharp for the tourists."

One of them is waving at us. "Hey Pogo! You coming back?"

I look at him.

"I told you I was the best," he says, jumping up and down. "Like a pogo stick."

I don't even know what a pogo stick is, but I don't tell him that. "I guess me and Frankie will head on out then. Let you guys get back to it."

"Come back around six or so," Pogo says. "You can watch us do our thing. These tourists, they eat this shit up, you know?"

"We might do that," I say, but I'm thinking I've already seen what they do. Not much reason to come back.

Chapter Sixteen

We get back over to Second Street and drive a few blocks, just checking out what Memphis is like. There's an open space with trees on the left and I find a place for the truck on a street close by. Frankie and I walk over to have a look. This is what they call a park in the city, I guess, but I still have a hard time calling it that after living next to the Smokies for my whole life.

There's a place called the Blue Plate that faces the park. It looks like the kind of place I might like to eat, no fancy stuff I've never heard of, but I'm pretty sure they won't let Frankie inside.

We're sitting out there and it looks like it's really popular. There's people going in and out all the time and every time the door opens we can smell bacon. I figure there's biscuits to go with that and who knows what else. After that bagel and whatever at Billie's I'm ready for some real breakfast, but I don't see any way to get in, and everything's so crowded here that I don't think I can get to a back door like I did at Interstate.

"It's a great place. Sometimes I come down here just for the aroma."

I look up and there's a woman standing there. She's older than me, maybe as old as Momma, but she doesn't look all beat down like Momma did. I stand up real quick and so does Frankie.

"What a polite dog," she says. "What's her name?"

I tell her and she bends over a little bit to say hi. Frankie is acting like she wants to jump right up in her lap.

She lets Frankie sniff the back of her hand and then gives her a scratch behind one ear. Then she straightens up and sticks out her hand. "Sorry, but I always say hello to the dog first. You can tell a lot about a person by how their dog acts, don't you think?" She smiles at me. "I don't believe I got your name. I'm Pam. Everybody calls me P. J."

"Boone," I say, and we shake.

"They won't let you in unless she's a service animal," P. J. says.

"I figured that."

"If you'll give me your order I'd be glad to get it to go and bring it out here."

Frankie's had plenty of dog food already, but all I had this morning was a handful of cereal.

"That would be great," I say, and reach for my

billfold.

"Oh, let me buy you breakfast," she says.

"If you don't mind, ma'am, I'd like to buy yours. You're doing us a big favor by getting us breakfast and bringing it out here. I'd feel a lot better if you'd let me pay for it."

She looks at me for a second and then nods. "If you insist, Boone. What would you like?"

I tell her I'm not sure what they have and it's pretty clear as soon as she starts talking that she's been here a lot.

"The omelets are wonderful, and they have a strawberry cream waffle that is incredible. You look like a carnivore to me, so I'm thinking a ham and cheese omelet with bacon and hash browns on the side. And maybe a side order of sausage biscuits so Frankie won't feel like she's left out." She stops for just a second. "Maybe some black coffee for you? I don't know whether they have anything for Frankie to drink or not."

"I've got a jug of water back at the truck," I say. I don't think she meant anything when she called me a carnivore, so I don't get too worked up about it. I've been called all kinds of names, but she didn't sound like she was being mean. Maybe she was joking a little bit. I still have a lot of trouble figuring out when people are doing that.

"All that sounds really good," I say. "What are you

205

going to have?" I ask just to be polite, but I don't mind when she doesn't answer me. I try to guess how much all that will be and decide too much is better than not enough.

I hand her a couple of twenties and she nods. "I think that will take care of everything with quite a bit to spare."

I start to tell her to keep the change but for some reason that feels like the wrong thing to say, like when I tried to pay that guy in New Orleans for the sandwich he gave me.

"I'll be back shortly," she says, and goes in right behind a couple of guys about my age. She talks to the woman at the cash register for a second and then looks out at me, smiles, and gives me a thumbs up. I think we're good.

She comes out with a bag and one of those paper holders with two cups, and I meet her a few steps out of the door and take the bag. It's pretty heavy and smells great. We find a spot to sit and eat, and I start unpacking the bag and laying things out.

I try the coffee first; it's nice and strong. Tastes different than at Cafe du Monde, but I think they have their own kind there. There's big chunks of ham in the omelet, but I try the bacon first. It's good, but it's not Benton's.

Looks like P. J. went for the waffle. I got to admit it looks pretty good. I don't eat a lot of sweet stuff unless it's dessert, but I could see trying that waffle sometime.

She takes a sip of her coffee. "So, Boone, are you visiting Memphis from close by? You don't sound like you're from here." Her plate is balanced on her lap and she starts in on the waffle.

I've got a mouthful of omelet, so I don't answer right away, but after another drink of coffee I tell her about Melvin and his map and a little about where I've been so far. Frankie is working on a sausage biscuit and isn't paying much attention to us at all.

"So, you're on vacation from your job at the senior facility?" She says "so" a lot; it's funny how I'm noticing people's habits more on this trip, like the guy at the rest stop on the way to the beach that nodded all the time. I wonder what kind of stuff I do that people think is weird.

That gets me thinking about the folks back home. Gamaliel used to rub his left cheek with his right hand. I never gave it any thought until just now. And Tiny, he had that short laugh he did all the time, even when things weren't funny. Nancy would twist her hair when she was thinking about something, and she had a bracelet she would turn back and forth on her arm. Deputy Anderson would put his thumbs in his back pockets; Frankie used to walk around right behind him, acting like a chicken. It was pretty funny, even when Anderson caught him in the act.

207

He tried to get all mad and give Frankie a lecture, but he couldn't do it. He got a kind of half grin on his face and just told him he better learn how to behave himself. Nobody could stay mad at Frankie.

P. J. clears her throat and I look over at her. "You were a thousand miles away, Boone," she says.

"Sorry." I shake my head. "Anyway, I'm not really on vacation. I sort of quit working there."

"What are you going to do when you get back?"

"Well, I'm not sure I'm going back," I say, but as soon as I say that I know it's not true. "I guess I will, though."

"So, you're not staying in Memphis? That's a shame. I know about a job you'd be perfect for if you were staying here."

I don't say anything, and she keeps talking.

"I volunteer at the animal shelter here two days a week, and they're looking for people to work with the animals. I can tell you're good with dogs; look how Frankie turned out. I think you'd be perfect for that kind of work."

She takes another sip. "I'm not interested myself; two days a week is plenty for me."

I take a bite of hash browns and tear the second biscuit in half. Frankie's watching me like a hawk, and when I start tearing up the sausage patty she starts whining real low.

P. J. laughs. "Don't you tease her now, Boone.

She's expecting to get at least some of that meat you're working on."

We eat and talk, and the food is gone in no time flat. Frankie gets both biscuits and the sausage. The omelet is huge, and that plus the bacon and hash browns is plenty for me. P. J. offers me a bite of the waffle, and it's really good. If I wasn't full already I would have asked her to go back in there and get one for me.

"So, how long are you going to be here?" She's putting everything back in the bag and looking around for a trash can. I take it from her and toss it in the can next to a statue of some guy. When I get back she's finishing up her coffee.

"Probably not much longer," I say. When I saw Beale Street earlier and thought about what it was going to be like full of people, I knew I wasn't going to go back to see Pogo and his friends. Melvin hadn't said I should do anything in Memphis except eat barbecue and see Beale Street and I've done both of those things. Just in case he left something out, I ask P. J. about it.

"Is there anything I ought to check out before I take off? I was thinking I might head back toward home before long, but if there's something else here I could stick around."

She looks at me. "Sounds like what you want to do is go back home sooner rather than later."

I don't say anything, and we sit there for a little bit watching the people go by. Then she clears her throat.

"My husband told me six months ago, when we were talking about vacations, that State Highway 70 goes all the way across the state from Memphis up to the Tri-Cities. It's a lot slower than the interstate, he said, but lots of pretty country and small towns."

She points back the way we came earlier in the day. "Union is just a block or two away from here. If you took that away from the river it would intersect with Summer on the other side of Memphis. Summer turns into Highway 70." She looks at me. "In case you didn't want to use 40."

I've been staring at the sidewalk, but I sit up straight and look over at her. I've looked at Melvin's map enough to know 40 is the interstate that heads back toward Knoxville. And out to California, but I'm sure not interested in going in that direction.

"Not that I'm trying to get you to leave," she says, and laughs. "It's really none of my business, Boone, but you look a little homesick."

I don't like it much that she's trying to tell me what I feel like, especially since she's right.

The thing is, at home even though I didn't have any friends or anything at least I knew my way around. Where things were, how to act, all that shit. I'm learning all kinds of stuff on this trip, but it's wearing me out.

And then there's Frankie.

She's the best thing that's happened to me since, well, since I don't know when. If I didn't have her I don't know what I would've done the last couple of years.

Going on this trip, though, having her along has been both good and bad. Most everybody I've met this past week I've met because of her. She's a good looking dog and knows how to behave herself, so people come up and ask about her. I sure never would have met Billie if her brother Louis hadn't asked me about Frankie and we got to talking.

Or Raymond and Charlotte either, as far as that goes. I mean, having Frankie next to me helped me chase off those assholes that were bothering Raymond at the swamp, and I got a good meal out of it. They were pretty interesting folks, too, and I'm glad I met them. That fruity moonshine was awful, but Raymond didn't know any better.

On the other hand, I might not have even been able to go to the beach if I hadn't run into that guy at the rest stop, the one who told me that some beaches don't allow dogs. Most of the Okefenokee Swamp didn't allow dogs, either, and New Orleans and Memphis both are mostly places where you need to be able to go inside to eat or listen to music or whatever. So Frankie kept me out of all that stuff.

I guess Melvin wasn't thinking about me taking Frankie along when he laid out this trip for me. Or if he was, he probably figured I'd leave her in the car or something if I had to. I might have done that except for my run-in with Abigail and her hammer. Man, was she mad. And that happened right at the beginning of this trip, so I never did anything that meant I'd have to leave Frankie.

I wouldn't trade her for anything, but I can't help wondering what this trip would have been like if I didn't have to worry about her.

Not nearly as good, I decide. So I need to stop thinking about it.

Frankie moves away from me a little and I look over at her. P. J.'s got her hand on Frankie's head and Frankie's got her eyes closed. Her tail is barely wagging.

P. J. grins at me. "I think your dog likes me."

I nod. "She's a pretty good judge of people. If she likes you, you must be okay."

She laughs out loud. "Well, thank you, Frankie, for the approval." She stands up. "If you've got the time, Boone, we could take a short walk around. I can tell you a little bit about Memphis. I've lived here for years; it's a pretty interesting place."

Chapter Seventeen

By the time we finish walking around I've seen the Pyramid, which has to be the weirdest damn building I've ever seen, and a big building called the FedEx Forum, where P. J. says you can see basketball games and concerts and some of the best tickets are $800.00 each, which I think is just crazy. I remember going down to Market Square with Nancy and how it didn't cost anything at all except for a place to park the car, and how much fun that was.

"You know people that would pay that kind of money to go to a ball game? Or a concert?"

She shakes her head. "So, as far as those real expensive tickets, some of the businesses in town buy a block of seats so they can entertain guests from out of town, clients, that kind of thing. And there are people who can afford to pay that kind of money and not even think about it."

I just look at her.

"It's like any city, Boone. There are people here

with a lot of money, and they can do things the rest of us can't. When we go we don't get the good seats. Some of the tickets, the ones we can afford, are only about $40 or $50 each."

I don't tell her that there's no way in hell I'd pay $50 for a ticket to anything.

By the time we make it back to the Blue Plate we've covered half a dozen blocks. I start to thank P. J. and tell her goodbye, but she's bending down whispering to Frankie. Then she stands up and looks at me.

"Frankie says she's never been out on a river before. Is that true, Boone?"

I don't know what to say to that, but she's not waiting for an answer.

"Let me call my husband. If he can get away early he can take us out on the Mississippi for a little while before it gets dark." She pulls out her cell phone.

I haven't looked at my phone for a few days. Probably I should do that, even though I'm pretty sure nobody's even noticed we're gone except Mark, and that's only because I left him that note.

Wonder if Tiny got that note to Nancy yet. I'll bet he hasn't; it's only been a few days. Seems like a lot longer than that. Hell, Stan might have shipped her off to college already, but I'd be surprised if he did. He was keeping a real close eye on her, and if she was off somewhere he couldn't. Plus I don't know whether or not Nancy would call me if she did have my number.

All of a sudden I'm thinking about Abigail, and then about Billie, and now I'm wondering if I even want Nancy to call me. I mean, if she really wanted to, she could have seen me or at least called me even with Stan all over her like he was. I was the one that tried to get a hold of her, and I never got anywhere with that.

P. J. had walked off a little ways, talking on her phone, and put it back in her pocket as she came toward us.

"So, you want to see the Mississippi River?" She's got a big grin on her face. "I caught my husband at the beginning of some meeting that he said he would skip out of as soon as he could. I wish our son could come along, but he's out of town, over in Nashville until next week. The three of us could go out for a little while, though. Sorry, Frankie, the four of us. Right?" She ruffles Frankie's fur and looks up at me.

I don't want to tell her I've never been out on a boat before, or that I can barely swim, but I've seen about as much city as I care to for a while. It's early afternoon now, and I haven't figured out what I'm doing next, so I say, "Sure. Let's go for a boat ride. Okay, Frankie?" She isn't even looking at me. She's too busy getting her head rubbed.

P. J. rides in my truck with Frankie in between us

and gives me directions to where their boat is. We walk down a steep hill and out over a short bridge that gets us to the marina. There are about a hundred boats, all in their own spaces under a big roof that must be twenty feet up. I know they've got marinas back home because I've seen the signs for them, but I never knew anybody that had a boat at one. Some of these damn boats are bigger than Gamaliel's house.

P. J. calls the place they keep their boat a slip which I think is a pretty weird name for it. Her husband is already there, walking around looking at everything.

His name is Joaquin. I know that's a Mexican name because of all those guys that worked the fields back home. Some of them had names like that. I remember how Daddy hated Mexicans, but they never bothered me any and Joaquin seems okay to me. He shows me around the boat and I'm thinking, if Raymond and Charlotte had a boat, it would be this one. It's got a bedroom and a kitchen and three places with chairs and tables so you can sit outside and eat or drink or fish or whatever, but this doesn't seem like the kind of boat you fish from.

He takes me up into the cockpit, which has got more dials and controls than any car I've ever seen. He leans over and shouts down at P. J. to cast off and she starts untying the ropes that are keeping the boat from floating off somewhere. Joaquin pushes a couple of buttons and I hear the engines start. He looks over at me and grins. "You will not believe the sunset out on the river, Boone." Then he moves out real slow, steering the boat out of the slip and past the other boats. There's a lot of other boats here.

Frankie is kind of freaked out when the boat starts moving and I go back down to hang onto her. Turns out I don't have to worry. P. J.'s got her and they're sitting out toward the front of the boat. Frankie looks okay until we get away from the marina and Joaquin floors it. The front part of the boat lifts up a little bit and we get the wind right in our faces. I sit down next to them, hook my finger into Frankie's collar, and look over at P. J.; she's got her eyes closed and this huge smile on her face.

It takes Frankie a minute to settle down after the boat starts really moving. That's a lot of new stuff all at once. The floor is moving, it's tilted, there's water all around us, everything except me is new. So it takes her a minute, but she figures it out. Then Joaquin calls down to P. J., "Life jackets!"

She gets up and opens a storage chest. "Here, Boone, put this on," and she tosses me a jacket. I watch her put hers on and figure it out from that. Then she says, "Would Frankie wear this?" She's holding up a thing that looks kind of like saddlebags. Frankie goes over and sniffs at it, and P. J. bends down and buckles it on.

"State law," she says. "Life jackets are required for everybody."

Frankie seems okay with it, which kind of surprises me. I'm glad, though. We're not even that far out into the river and it's the biggest damn thing I've ever seen. Joaquin yells down from the cockpit, "Hey, Boone! Look at that barge!" He's pointing off to the right.

It looks like it's about a mile long. It seems like it's barely moving, but I can tell even from here that if you got in its way you were gone. Now I'm wishing I had a leash for Frankie. If she jumped off the boat and got caught in front of that thing I'd never find her.

Joaquin turns so we're running beside it going in the opposite direction. He stays pretty far away, a good hundred feet or so, but we're still bobbing up and down. Damn thing goes on forever, but finally it's past us and heading on up the river.

The afternoon is real comfortable out on the river. P. J. hands around bottles of some kind of beer I've never heard of and we sit around and eat pretzels and drink beer and watch the traffic on the river. The sunset is different than at home, everything's so flat here, but it is a beauty. I understand why they wanted to bring me out here. This is pretty damn good.

When we get back to the marina Joaquin backs it in to its slip and I try to help with the ropes. They don't really need me, I can tell. They've probably done this a bunch of times before, but they act like they appreciate me pitching in.

Joaquin pulls me aside while we're walking up to the cars. "She's going to ask you to come to our house for supper. Just thought I'd warn you."

I don't say anything. I'd been trying to decide whether I wanted to stick around Memphis for another day or start back toward home.

"She really likes Frankie, Boone," he says. "If it wouldn't mess up your travels too much, we'll . . ." He stops talking when P. J. slows down so she's walking beside us.

Sure enough, she does just what Joaquin said she would do. I'm glad he warned me.

"Sure," I say. "I was going to head on back east, but I can just as easy do that later on tonight."

The meal is good, nothing fancy, but I'm finding out on this trip that I don't like fancy food too much. She asks me to put off starting my trip back until tomorrow, but when I say I like driving at night and I'd just as soon get started, she nods her head. I can tell she's disappointed, but she doesn't make a big deal out of it. She gives me her cell number and makes me promise to call and let them know how I'm doing. I tell her sure, but I don't know if I'll actually do that. I say yes just so I can get out of there.

Truth is, I've never driven much at night, and especially not on roads I've never been on before, but the more I think about heading home the more I want to get started.

Joaquin starts to give me directions and she looks at him like, are you crazy? and he laughs and says, "Right. I'd just get him lost. Come on, Boone, you can follow me. I'll get you to Highway 70. It's not too far from here, and you won't have to go back into town and figure out all the turns."

I say thanks and I'm about to head out the door behind him when P. J. says, "Hold on a second." She bends down and whispers something to Frankie and then, when she stands up, throws her arms around me and gives me a big hug. I didn't see that coming so I end up just standing there. She lets go after a second and says, "You two have a safe trip back, and, Boone, think about what I said about working with animals. I've got a feeling about you. I think you'd be great."

I'm still just standing there like an idiot and finally I mumble something about being sure to do that, and thanks for the boat ride and the meal. Then I get me and Frankie out of there as quick as I can. I feel like I'm about to start crying, and I don't know why.

Chapter Eighteen

It's pretty clear about a half hour into the trip that starting out at night is a bad idea.

The main reason is I'm on roads I've never seen before. Back home, there were some roads I could just about drive with my eyes closed, so driving at night was no big deal.

Here, after I almost missed a curve and just about drove through an intersection instead of turning right to stay on 70, I decide to find a place to pull over and wait until morning.

"Should have stayed with them, I guess," I tell Frankie. "I'm not gaining any time doing it this way."

I find a U-Haul store right on the highway and pull in beside the building. There's nobody around, and I figure I'll get a few hours sleep and take off as soon as it's light. I'd like to be gone before they open tomorrow morning, whenever that is.

After I get Frankie some water and walk her around a little, I put her in the back and dig the phone out of the glove compartment. I don't figure anybody has tried to call, but I check anyway.

There are four missed calls.

It takes me a second to remember what the guy showed me when I bought the phone about how to check for messages. Three of the calls are just hangups, but the last one has a voicemail.

"Hey, it's Tiny. I saw Nancy and gave her your note, but when I told her you were gone and I wasn't sure when you were coming back she wadded it up and tossed it. Said she didn't care if she never saw you again. Well, anyway, I figured you ought to know. Sorry, man."

Great.

At first I'm really pissed off. I mean, I tried to talk to her at the grocery store, I tried to call her, it's not like I just took off. Did she try to get hold of me? Not once. Not a call, a note, a call from one of her friends, not a damn thing. Plus, she didn't even read the note I left for her. Tiny said she threw it away like it was trash. I mean, for a while there I was even going to ask her to come with me on this trip. Having her along was going to make the trip so much better.

The more I think about that, though, the more I'm glad she didn't. I might have still met Raymond and Charlotte, and P. J. and Joaquin, but I sure wouldn't have met Abigail, or Jericho, or Louis, or his sister Billie. And meeting Billie has been worth the whole trip so far.

Probably better that Nancy didn't come. Not that she would have if I could have asked her, with her going off to college and all. She might be there already, wherever there is. I bet she's got her eye on some college guy already.

I listen to the voicemail again. Still a little mad, but now I'm thinking maybe I don't care if I never see her again, either.

The next morning I'm up and out of there in plenty of time. Nobody in the lot, and really nobody on the road. There's a minute at first when I think about heading west and trying to find P. J. and Joaquin, or back to New Orleans to track down Billie, but that doesn't last long at all. I have no idea how I would even start, and even though what Nancy did still has me pissed off a little, I've already decided that she can do whatever the hell she wants and I'll do the same. Even with all that, heading back to East Tennessee still feels like the right decision. So I'm going east, and what I'm thinking is that I might as well drive straight through. I've seen enough new stuff for one trip.

Nashville turns out to be a lot less awful than I thought it was going to be. 70 turns into West End and then Broadway, and then I hit a river and have to turn one way or the other. I make a guess and turn right, and before too long I'm on the other side of the city.

It's still kind of flat, but not like it was the other side of Nashville. I come to a split not too long after leaving the city and have to decide between 70N and 70. I don't think I want to go north, so I take 70.

I drive through a Hardee's in Smithville and get a couple of burgers, one order of large fries, and a large coke. There's an empty lot just past it and I pull in so we can eat and Frankie can pee.

After that it all changes pretty fast. Before I know it I'm in mountains again. Not the Smokies, it's too soon for that, but it's starting to feel like home. I pass through Rockwood coming down into the valley and then I'm coming up on Knoxville and I can see the Smokies up ahead. They're still pretty far off, but it sure is good to see them.

I'm still south of Knoxville when I find an old gas station that looks like it's been closed for ten or fifteen years and pull into the parking lot. I had been thinking I'd just get through Knoxville and go on home, be there in time to maybe get something to eat, and then I remember I don't have a place to go. I quit my job at the home, our old house is probably about half fallen down, and Gamaliel's old place belongs to Carrie now. Who knows what she's planning to do with it. Probably sell it or rent it out, and even if she hasn't done anything yet, she was really pissed at me the last time I saw her.

Maybe I'll go by the home and say hi to Mark and Melvin. It's coming on dark, though, and I bet Mark's gone for the day and Melvin might already be asleep.

"Well, Frankie, this kind of sucks, doesn't it?" I look over at her.

I'm trying to remember why I was so damn anxious to get back. I could still be in Memphis. Hell, I could have a job in Memphis, if P. J. was right about that animal shelter. Or I could be in New Orleans with Billie. As soon as I think that, though, I know that's not real. When she dropped me off at Bourbon Street it wasn't a see you later kind of thing. It was goodbye.

The Memphis thing, though, that might have actually happened if I'd been willing to check out the animal shelter job. I bet P. J. and Joaquin would have put me up for a while until I got a place of my own.

Why the hell was I so bound and determined to get back here?

I get Melvin's map back out and unfold it. Then I fold it back up and put it back in the glove compartment. As long as I'm this close, I'll stop by the home tomorrow and see Mark and Melvin. And I'll give Tiny a call, see what he's up to. Hell, maybe I'll do that right now. I get the phone out and see that I've had another call.

It's another hangup, and since I don't really know

225

anybody's number I don't recognize it. And there's no voicemail, either, so I just forget about it and call Tiny.

It rings a few times before he answers it.

"Boone, how in the hell are you, man?"

"I'm good. We're good."

"I got to say, I figured I'd hear from you right after I left that voicemail."

"Yeah, I just played it late last night. Forgot to check the phone."

He's quiet for a half a minute.

"Nobody left you any other messages?"

"No, man. Just yours. Kind of pissed me off, but I'm pretty much over it now."

"Well, the reason I asked, I thought I saw her circle back, you know, after she tossed it, and pick it back up, but I guess not."

"I guess not."

Neither one of us says anything for a minute.

"So, where are you? I didn't even know where you were going."

"Yeah, I didn't either."

He laughs that short laugh of his.

"Right. So are you out West somewhere? On a beach watching all the fine women? Mexico?"

"I'm about an hour south of you, give or take."

"No shit? You're already back?"

"Yeah, didn't really have a plan, like I said, and I

just ended up heading back this way. I don't know how long I'm staying, though."

That's not right, and I know it as soon as I say it.

"Shit, man, if I ever get out of here I'm not ever coming back."

"Well, I probably won't stay long. Still a lot of stuff to see, you know?"

"Listen, man, you can't take off again without coming by, all right?"

I nod and then remember to say, "Definitely."

"So, listen," he says. "I got to get back inside. I got nothing going on tomorrow, so you better get your ass up here and tell me about all the trouble you got into out there. I guarantee you got into some shit, right?"

"Well," I say.

I'm grinning like a fool thinking about what all I can tell Tiny about. He's not going to believe me about Billie. Sometimes I can't believe it, and I was there.

"That's what I thought," he says. I hear the door open and somebody says, "Tiny, get back in here! You're up!"

"I gotta go, Boone. Tomorrow, man."

I start to say something, but he's already hung up on me.

Chapter Nineteen

The morning starts off really good. I get started early and make it past Knoxville without too much trouble. I get back to the old folk's home and drive into the parking lot about a minute ahead of Mark, so I'm just putting Frankie on her leash when he pulls in.

He parks that little Mini across from us, jumps out, and spreads his arms wide.

"What a wonderful surprise! When did you get back, Boone? Good morning, Frankie!"

Frankie is pulling so hard I can barely hang on to her. I'm about to have to turn her loose when Mark gets close enough to reach down and scratch the top of Frankie's head.

That satisfies her for a minute and he comes up to me. I start to stick out my hand and he grabs me in a hug that I didn't expect, but I have to admit feels pretty good.

He steps back but keeps his hand resting on my

shoulder. "I was thinking about you and Frankie yesterday. Do you have a little time to visit? I know everybody here would love to see you."

"You mean see Frankie," I say, but I've got a big smile on my face.

"Well, of course," Mark says. "We all know who the star is, right, Frankie?"

Frankie must really have missed Mark, the way she's acting. We've only been gone about two weeks, and she's acting like it's been years.

"Come on," says Mark. "We'll surprise Betty."

"I want to see Melvin, for sure," I say, and Mark stops. He turns around and looks at me.

"It's a good thing you came back by, Boone. I'm afraid Melvin is moving to hospice next week. I know he'll be glad to see you, and if you had waited a couple of weeks you might have missed him." He starts walking again and says, over his shoulder, "His cancer just keeps coming back."

I follow Mark in through the side entrance and into his office. The jar of shine is sitting on the top shelf of his bookcase. Looks like it's about three quarters full.

He sees me looking. "Thanks for that, Boone, although it's not the kind of gift I usually get. Very smooth. I'm not sure I want to know the story behind that jar." He smiles a little, and picks up the phone without sitting down.

"Betty? Can you come by my office for a second? I just got in and found something in the parking lot I think you should take a look at." He winks at me. "Five minutes? Great."

I'm not sure I want to see her, since she was so mad at me about Nancy, but when she gets to the office she does the same thing Mark did, gives me a big hug, and makes a big fuss over Frankie.

I tell them about Caswell Beach, and Jericho, and Raymond and Charlotte, and P. J. and Joaquin over in Memphis, but not about Billie. I don't feel right talking about that with these two.

When I tell Betty I want to see Melvin she looks over at Mark and he nods.

"So you know about the cancer?"

"Yeah. I hate that."

"Oh, Boone, so do we. He's such a delight. We will miss him. But let's go down there right now and surprise him. I'm sure he's back from breakfast and he will absolutely love to see you." She starts to leave and stops at the door. "I believe he knew the prognosis before you left. I'm not surprised he didn't tell you. That's so like him. What a dear, dear man."

So we go and surprise him, and after a minute Mark and Betty excuse themselves and it's just me and Melvin and Frankie in his room.

"So, young man, you must tell me everything about your trip." He shakes a finger at me. "Don't leave anything out, now."

I'm not sure how he knows to say that, but I figure he can keep a secret if I ask him to. It just doesn't seem right talking to Mark and Betty about Billie and her family, but I got to tell somebody and I figure Melvin will appreciate it.

So I tell him about Abigail and Jericho and the assholes at the swamp, and Raymond and Charlotte, and the pickpockets on Bourbon Street, and he stops me over and over to ask me questions about what I saw and where I ate and all kinds of stuff.

When I get to the part about the Armstrong family and their gumbo and pecan pie, he leans back in his bed and closes his eyes. He has a little smile on his face and doesn't ask any questions, just listens. As soon as I start talking about Billie giving me a ride back to my truck his eyes open and he straightens up a little bit, and when I get to where she's taking me home with her he holds up his hand.

"Don't rush through this part, Boone." He grins. "Was this your first time?"

I want to tell him that it's none of his damn business, but I don't. If he hadn't sent me on this trip, practically pushed me out the door, I wouldn't have had one of the best weeks of my life. Maybe the best. I guess I owe him a good story.

So I tell him about Billie, and about Memphis and what all I did there, and about my trip back across the state, and when I say, "I got back about an hour ago and just wanted to come by and say thanks for giving me the map and all the suggestions. It was a great trip," he laughs out loud. Shaking his finger at me, he starts to say something, and can't because he starts laughing again and pretty soon I'm laughing, too. It takes us a minute or two to get ourselves stopped.

"Boone," he says, "that is without a doubt the best going away present I could have gotten. Now, don't pretend they didn't tell you," he says when he sees the look on my face. "I know I'm almost done here. I'm at peace with that. You have given me a good laugh and some great stories, and I couldn't ask for a better gift."

I don't know what to say to that. A minute ago I was laughing and now I'm tearing up. Melvin puts his hand out and I shake it, easy because I don't want to hurt him, and he says, "If you don't mind, Boone, I'm a little tired. I think I'll take a nap. Frankie, you beautiful girl, come over here and tell me goodbye now."

Frankie trots over and sticks her nose up into his hand, and he lets it rest there for a second.

Then he pulls his hand back. "All right, Boone, thank you for stopping by. It was a lovely visit, just lovely." He gives me a little smile. "What was it your young lady said to you? Buckle your seat belt, it's

233

going to be a bumpy ride? Do you know the reference?"

I shake my head. I remember when she said it and I buckled my belt, I looked over at Billie and she was looking at me kind of funny. "It's from a movie," Melvin says. "Not an exact quote, and a little out of context, but she was telling you to get ready for what was about to happen."

He laughs again and waves me out of the room.

Chapter Twenty

First Gamaliel and now Melvin. I don't know what it is about me and old guys, but we seem to get along real well. I guess the other side of that is the short time they've got left. It really sucks. I had planned to spend some time with Mark, but now I just want to get the hell out of here. I know I need to check in with him before I go, though, so I head down the hall to his end of the building.

When I get to Mark's office he's sitting at his desk staring a a picture on his wall. He sees me at the door and motions me in. I close the door behind me and sit where I usually do. He turns to face me.

"How was your visit with Melvin?"

I can feel the tears start down my cheeks and I reach up to wipe them off. Frankie scoots over next to me and does that real soft whine that says she's worried. I put my hand on her head and leave it there.

While I'm getting myself back together I think

about how to answer Mark. Part of me wants to say, "It was fucked up. Don't know why you even need to ask me that stupid question," and part of me wants to tell him how grateful Melvin was for the stories of my trip, I guess because they took his mind off him dying and all. And part of me wants to just get up and walk back out the door, but I know I'm not going to do that.

I take a couple of deep breaths and say, "What's the deal with that picture you were looking at?"

He looks at me for a second and then nods. I guess he's figured out I don't want to talk about Melvin.

He stands up. "Come over here, Boone." He walks over to the picture and I go over and stand beside him.

It's really a whole bunch of pictures all in the same frame. They're all pictures of people; some of them are young, like my age, and some of them look like they're a hundred years old.

"My brother gave this to me as a graduation gift when I finished seminary," he says.

I didn't even know Mark had a brother.

Actually I don't know hardly anything about Mark. He knows a hell of a lot about me, though, and I guess it's the way it is. Preachers end up knowing all kinds of shit about people. Most of it bad stuff, too, because that's what people talk to preachers about, the bad stuff they've done or that somebody's done to them. That's a lot of stuff to carry around, and a lot of secrets to keep. I look over at Mark, thinking, there's no way in hell I'd want his job.

"So," he says, "this is my grandfather," he points to a picture up in the left corner, "and that guy with him was his best friend. Reginald was his name. Awfully fancy name for just a regular guy, but he never wanted anybody to shorten it to Reggie or anything like that.

"He died a few years before Pops did, and it was at the funeral that we found out why it seemed like he never had any money. That church was packed to the roof with people none of us had ever seen before, and they all had a story about how Reginald had loaned them a car payment, or just gave them enough money to fill their tank, the stories went on and on. None of us that knew him ever really did, as it turns out. He touched so many lives."

Mark stops for a second and then goes on. "I could tell you the same kind of story about every one of these people. Some of them were my family, my neighbors, some of them were the folks that reached out to me or my family. They all, every one of them, just went about their lives, doing good, reaching people, and never spent a minute thinking about getting credit or being noticed."

He looks at me and then back at the picture.

"When I went into seminary, my family was

surprised, except my brother Jules. He acted like, well, of course Mark's going to be a preacher. Then, at the dinner my parents gave me when I graduated, he called me up into our bedroom, the one we shared when we were kids, and gave me this. Told me the story of every one of these fine people. He said, 'Mark, you're going to hear a lot about the worst side of people. I thought you ought to have a reminder of the best side to kind of balance that out.' I remember saying thank you, not realizing at the time that this is, without a doubt, the best thing anyone has ever given me."

He sits back down at his desk and I stay at the picture for another minute, looking at all those people. I don't know how Mark knew what I was thinking, about never wanting his job, but it sure feels like he knew.

When I sit back down he looks at me for a long time.

"I've been thinking about you a lot since you left. You're a fine young man, Boone," he says. "It's about time for you to start considering what you want to do next, if you haven't already."

Now he sounds like Raymond and that whole "do something useful" stuff.

"I just want you to think about the reason my brother gave me that picture. None of those people had any notion of doing big things, or great things,

238

they just looked at what was right in front of them and, when they saw the chance, did the right thing."

He doesn't have to worry about me having any kind of notion of doing great things, that's for sure. I'm still just trying not to turn out like my daddy, and it's like I can't get rid of all that nasty shit he put in my head. I mean, if I could figure out how not to be an asshole I'd feel like I was ahead of the game.

I don't say any of that to Mark.

"Listen, Mark, I got to go. I told Tiny I'd come by to see him today, and I'll have to track him down."

He nods. "I understand, Boone, of course. And what about Nancy?"

"I don't want to talk about her."

He takes a breath. "I see."

We both just sit there. I'm looking everywhere but at him.

"Well," he finally says, "I should probably get to work here."

I can't tell whether he's pissed off at me, or he's giving me an excuse to get out of here.

I stand up. "Listen, Mark, I . . . . You'll let me know about Melvin, right?"

"Of course."

I start to say something else and he cuts me off. He points to the picture. "It's my goal in life to be worthy of being included in that collage. There's a place for you up there too, Boone. The work you and

Frankie did with these people here," he waves his hand toward the hallway, "you have no idea what a difference you have already made in your short life. I'd bet that Melvin is reliving your visit right now, treasuring every moment of it."

I say the only thing I can think of. "You know, Mark, you just can't help but talk like a preacher, can you?" He gives me a look and then realizes I'm just giving him a hard time. He smiles a little and shrugs his shoulders.

"I know, I know, and it's not even Sunday. Get out of here, Boone, and let me get to work."

Chapter Twenty-One

Betty is standing at the edge of the parking lot talking on her phone, but hangs up when she sees me and meets me at the truck.

"It's good to see you and Frankie, Boone," she says. "All the residents here ask about you two. If you are going to be in town for a while, give me a call. I have a couple of things I want to talk to you about."

She starts to say something else and her phone goes off and she looks at the number. "I need to take this, Boone. Sorry." She walks away and I can't hear anything she's saying. From the way she's talking it's something serious, though.

I get Frankie in the truck and go around to my side. We pull out onto the road and head toward Tiny's farm. There's a place I can drive through and get us something to eat, and I can call Tiny from the lot. I'm not sure what Betty might have in mind, but I figure I'll think about it later.

Tiny says he's got some friends coming over to

241

grill burgers and shoot the shit and that I should come by about five or so. I tell him we'll be there.

We eat and head over to the bank. I've still got most of that money Raymond gave me, since he or Charlotte paid for the window replacement back in Georgia. It feels weird to come back from a trip with more money than I left with, but if I'm telling the truth, it feels weird to go on a trip at all.

When Daddy was alive and the family was still together, we never even thought about going anywhere. I think I remember going to see some of Daddy's people when me and Frankie and Hannah were real little, but I'm not even sure that's not something I just dreamed.

I mean, I understand about money being tight and all, with Daddy having to take whatever job he could get. He didn't know how to do much of anything, so mostly he did the kind of shit work anybody with a strong back could do, the kind of a job where it didn't matter if you were smart or dumb as a rock as long as you could take orders and pull your weight.

It was the taking orders part that cost him one job after another, so he never stayed anywhere long enough to get a raise or a promotion. Maybe that was for the best, though. If he got to be a manager of some kind I'd hate to have been the guy taking orders from him. He was a scary guy sometimes. At least he was with us.

I have to park at the bank and dig around in the glove compartment before I go through the drive through window. I've never made a deposit that way, so I'm not sure what all they are going to want. So I pile up everything I can think of in my lap and wait until there's nobody in line.

The guy on the other side of the glass looks kind of familiar but I can't figure out who it is. He tells me what I need to put in the drawer and when I do, he glances at my name and says, "Boone Hammond?"

I nod.

"You got a dog from my younger brother Gary a while back. Pitiful little thing, if I remember. Dad was going to get rid of it."

I lean back so he can see Frankie.

"That's her?" he says. "Damn, she turned out to be a beauty!"

Some woman with a real sour expression on her face comes up and says, "Excuse me, sir, is there a problem?"

"No," I say, wondering what the hell she's talking about.

"Well," she says, giving Gary's brother a dirty look, "On behalf of the bank I'd like to apologize for the language our teller used. I'll be speaking to him later, you can be certain."

"Ma'am, I'm not worried about it," I say. "I'm a friend of his younger brother, and I just told him

243

something that really surprised him, is all. You don't need to speak to him on my account."

She doesn't say anything, just walks off.

The guy looks at me. "Thanks for trying, man, but she's, well, I should probably just talk to you about bank business. I've made your deposit. Will there be anything else you need?"

"No, I'm good," I say.

"Well, then, here's your receipt. You have a nice day, sir, and come back real soon."

He looks miserable; I guess he's going to get his ass chewed on his next break. I tell him thanks and drive on out of there.

I've got some time to kill until I head up to Tiny's place, so I drive up to Gamaliel's house. When I drive by our old place, I slow down to have a look. It's still standing, and doesn't really look much different than it did a couple of years ago when I lived there. There is an old pickup truck in the front yard, so I don't pull in. The only thing I'm curious about is the grave out back. I'm pretty sure it's deep enough that they could plow over it if anybody ever decided to do anything with the field. It's really shitty soil, though, so I can't see it being used for anything but hay.

Gamaliel's old place looks the same except for the "For Sale" sign out next to the road. There's nobody around, so I pull into the yard and Frankie and I get out. I don't bother with the leash; we both know this land real well. She's off like a shot sniffing around, and circles back to me about the time I start walking back into the woods.

The trail to where the still used to be is just about gone. It's so grown up I have trouble finding my way, but I keep going until I get to where I think the property line is. Part of me wants to go on over and sit by the pool for a while, but I don't. All that seems like a long time ago, and I don't want any more reminders of what it was like to live there.

"Frankie! Come on, girl, this was a bad idea," I say, and we make our way back down to the house. I peek inside the toolshed and it's empty. Nothing on any of the shelves, nothing on the floor. I guess since Carrie's selling the place she had to get everything out of there. I wonder what she did with it all. I bet the house is empty too.

Frankie's still nosing around like she's looking for Gamaliel. I'm probably just making that up, but it's one more reason to get the hell out of here. We get into the truck and pull out onto the road, heading back toward town.

By the time I get gas for the truck it's getting close to 5:00, so I head over toward Tiny's place. When I get there there's already two cars besides the ones that belong to the Thompsons. I don't recognize either one of them, but I know Tiny's got a lot of friends, so I'm not surprised.

Tiny is in the backyard, sitting in one of those folding chairs that have places in the arms for a can of beer or whatever. He's got a plastic cup in his hand and when he sees me he gets up and heads toward the picnic table.

"Get your skinny ass over here, Boone," he says, and points to a big metal washtub full of ice. "There's a couple of different kinds of beer in there," and he steps closer to me so he can talk softer, "and a can or two of Thunderstorm Soda. If you want an S&S I can fix you right up, but Mom's in the house so I can't have it sitting out here."

"What are you drinking?"

"Peyton brought a bottle of bourbon, so I'm having an S&W," he winks at me, "whiskey instead of shine. Our stuff is for special occasions."

"S&W sounds good to me."

"Okay. I'll make you one while I'm topping mine off." Tiny points toward the grill. "See those two guys that look kind of alike? They're brothers, two years apart. Peyton and Archie. Their dad's crazy about football."

I don't tell him that those names don't mean anything to me.

"That's Jill next to Peyton, and Miranda over there by Archie. The guy standing by my truck is Neil. Hey, guys!" he shouts and everybody turns toward us. "This is Boone, the guy I was telling you

246

about."

They all wave and go back to what they were doing except for Archie. He comes over to us and Miranda stays where she is for a second and then follows him.

Archie sticks out his hand and I shake it. When she gets close enough Miranda does the same thing, but it's like she's just copying Archie, not like she gives a damn one way or another that I'm there.

"So, Boone, Tiny tells us you're some kind of badass," Archie says. I look over at Tiny. He shrugs his shoulders and says, "Well, you didn't want me to lie to them, did you?"

I turn back to Archie. "I don't know about all that." I'm hoping he doesn't plan to do something stupid to show off for Miranda.

"Show him the scar," Tiny says.

Great. Now Tiny's egging him on.

"Which one?" I say before I think about it.

"Whoa," says Archie. "There's more than one?"

"Hey, Tiny," I say. "Where's that drink you were fixing for me?"

"Working on it," he says. "Show them the knife scar. I was there for that one, remember?"

"I remember you saved my ass," I say.

"Shit," says Tiny. "I just hurried him out the door a little. You were doing fine, considering he had a blade and you didn't."

Tiny hands me a drink and starts telling Archie about the fight with Jerry, except he makes Jerry sound like some kind of professional assassin and me sound like a, well, like a badass. Peyton and the other two drift over in time to hear most of it and Neil says, "Okay, let's see it."

I pull up my sleeve and they all look, and Peyton says, "Not very big, is it?" and everybody looks at me. I give him a big grin and say, "I tried to tell y'all it wasn't any big deal." I look over at Tiny. "You tell a great story, man. You almost had me kicking his ass all the way down to the Georgia state line." I start laughing and Tiny does, too, and then they all are, and before long they're on to talking about something else and nobody's paying attention to me. Which is just the way I want it. I haven't thought about Jerry in a while and don't like thinking about him now.

Frankie comes trotting up with Eunuch. I bend down and scratch him behind the ears. "Hey, boy, have you forgiven Tiny yet?"

"Don't get him started on me again, Boone," says Tiny. "He doesn't think about his missing balls at all until some asshole reminds him." He grins at me. "Has Frankie forgiven you?"

I wave him off. "That stuff was all inside of her. She doesn't even miss it. Poor Eunuch can't even lick his own balls anymore. If you ask me, that's pretty cruel, man."

I hear somebody laugh and look behind me.

Jill is wiping her chin. "Dammit, Boone, you made me spit out my beer!" Peyton comes over to see what's going on.

"What's so funny?"

Jill points at me. "He was giving Tiny shit about having Eunuch neutered and I overheard him. Lost a whole mouthful of beer. It's dripping down my chin, see?" She sticks her chin out toward Peyton.

He leans over and licks her face. "Yeah, that's beer all right."

She rolls her eyes. "You are disgusting." She doesn't sound disgusted.

"Damn, Peyton, you're starting kind of early," says Tiny.

Peyton grins at him. "No sense in wasting time. Right, Boone?" He looks over at me.

I just raise my glass to him, and he seems okay with that.

Which is good, because I still don't know how to joke around with people. I mean, I can with Tiny, he's different. It's like we understand each other. I don't know any of these people and I figure the chances are pretty good that I'll say something stupid before the day's over. Somebody'll say something funny and I won't know it's a joke, or they'll say something serious and I'll laugh when I'm not supposed to.

Tiny gets the grill started and Mrs. Thompson

shows up with a plate of hamburgers and a pile of cheese slices. "I'll bring out the rest of the stuff later," she says. She turns to go back in and sees me.

"Boone, how nice to see you! How are you doing these days?" She doesn't come over and hug me or anything, which is good, but she's smiling like she's really happy to see me.

"I'm fine, Mrs. Thompson. I appreciate you having me up here. How are you doing?"

She glances over at Tiny. "I didn't make the list, but I am glad you're on it. How's Frankie?"

"She's good. She's around here somewhere with Eunuch," I say.

"That name," she says, and I swear she looks kind of embarrassed. "I tried to get him to change it, but he wouldn't." She shakes her head. "Well, I'm glad to see you, Boone. Don't you be such a stranger, okay?"

"Yes, ma'am."

She goes back inside, and Neil says, "Yes, ma'am," in a kind of sarcastic voice.

I start to turn toward him and Tiny says, "Hey Boone, how about helping me out with these?"

He holds up the plate of burgers and cocks his head toward the grill. I shrug and follow him over.

"Don't pay any attention to Neil," he says, kind of low. "He gets a kick out of saying shit like that to see what people will do. If he can get to you he'll just keep at it. Like picking at a scab, you know?" He picks up a wire brush and cleans off the grill.

If that's what Neil does for fun I'm not sure why Tiny invited him to this thing, but I figure it's none of my business. Tiny lays the burgers out on the grill and picks up a long-handled spatula. "Now listen up, everybody," he says in a big voice. "I'm taking orders, so let me know how you like your burger. Bloody or burnt, or somewhere in between. This meat was walking around in our field about a week ago, so it's as fresh as you can get. We got two kinds of cheese, American and hot pepper, and Mom's got all the tomatoes and shit like that coming out in a minute."

He looks over at Archie. "Archie, you're in charge of making sure nobody runs dry. Okay?" Archie gives him a thumbs up and walks over to the table where the drinks are.

Half an hour later we're sitting around the big picnic table building our burgers. Mrs. Thompson had come out a few minutes before the burgers came off the grill and left a big platter with onions, lettuce, and tomatoes. There are four bags of chips and three different kinds of dip. Nobody says anything for a couple of minutes while we're getting our plates ready. I find a spot on the end to sit and call Frankie over. Tiny gets up, goes to the grill, and comes back with a half of a burger on his spatula.

"This one's Frankie's," he says. "The other half belongs to Eunuch."

"Thanks, man."

I break up the meat and put it on a little paper saucer. When I set it down in front of Frankie she sniffs it a couple of times and then inhales it. She looks up at me like, "Okay, where's the rest of it?"

"She's still hungry, isn't she?"

Jill is sitting more or less across from me.

I nod. "Some days I can't fill her up to save me."

She breaks off a little of hers. "This is too much for me anyway." She throws it at me and laughs when I almost fall off the bench trying to catch it.

"Frankie says thanks," I say, and tear it up a little before I put it on the saucer.

After I finish everything on my plate I say, "Tiny, I had a lot of really good food out on the road the last couple of weeks, but I got to say, your burger really kicks ass." I hold up my plate and Frankie's saucer.

Everybody else tells him how good it was, and he acts like it's just what he does all the time. I can tell he likes hearing that stuff, though. I guess I would too.

Jill looks across the table at me. "So what kind of food did you eat, wherever it was you went?"

"Yeah," says Tiny. "I want to hear about this trip. Where all did you end up going?"

I start to says something and Miranda says, "Let's move over to the patio. Archie and I were over there earlier, and the chairs are really comfortable."

"Yeah, I saw y'all over there," says Neil. "I was about to tell you to get a room." He laughs, but nobody else does.

We all grab chairs and Tiny says, "Okay, Boone, let's hear it."

I tell them about Melvin's map and how he had a bunch of places circled, and how the only thing I knew when we started was that I was going to try to get to as many places as I could. I told them about Abigail almost breaking out the window of my truck to rescue Frankie, and about Benton's bacon. Peyton says he's tried it once, and when I told him what Abigail said about it being better than sex, he looks at Jill and grins. "No comment."

None of them had ever had a low country boil and when I told them about just dumping all that food out of the big strainer onto a table, Tiny says, "Okay, that's the next meal we're doing up here."

I tell them about the three assholes at the Okefenokee Swamp, and about Raymond and Charlotte and the steak dinner I had with them. When I get to the part about the fruity moonshine Tiny laughs and starts to say something, then stops. But I can tell from the way he's looking at me what he wants to say.

I tell them about the pickpockets in New Orleans and about how delicious beignets are, and about meeting Louis and his family and getting invited to their house for gumbo and pecan pie.

The run through Mississippi was pretty boring so I skip to the Interstate Barbecue and meeting P. J. and Joaquin and going out on their boat.

Miranda gets up and says, "I'm about to bust. I got to go to the bathroom. Jill, you need to go?"

Jill gets up and the two girls head off into the house. As soon as they're out of hearing Tiny says, "Okay, Boone, what else happened?"

I look at him. "What are you talking about?"

"Come on, man. You're leaving something out. I know you, right?"

"I bet you got laid." Archie looks around. "I mean, he's told us about half a dozen women he met. Women and food, that's all you've talked about. Except for facing down those three guys in Georgia."

Tiny's been watching me and his grin gets bigger and bigger. "You know, Archie, I think you might be on to something. What about it, Boone?"

I try as hard as I can to keep the smile off my face, but I can't.

"I knew it!" Tiny slaps his hand down on the chair arm. "You got to tell us now, man, you know you do."

"Yeah," says Neil. "You can make something up, right?" He looks at me and smiles.

Tiny shakes his head. "Give it a rest, Neil." He turns to me. "Okay, man, hurry it up. The girls'll be back soon and we can't talk in front of them."

I look over at Neil until I catch his eye. "Here's something for you to dream about, Neil."

"Frankie kind of introduced us," I say, and tell them about meeting Louis in the park and getting the invitation to eat at his mom's house. I tell them about meeting Miles, and Charlie, and Billie, and how Billie kept looking at me all during dinner. How she offered me a ride back to my truck after I almost got myself in trouble with Miles, and how Frankie wouldn't get out of her car when we got back to Bourbon Street.

"So she says, buckle your seat belt, it's going to be a bumpy night," I say, and I have to smile just remembering, "and it was that. She was the most beautiful thing I've ever seen, and she —"

"What are you guys talking about?" Miranda and Jill walk up to where we're sitting.

"Boone was just telling us about getting laid," Neil says. He looks over at me. "It sounds to me like this little piece of ass was an Afro-American. Is that right?" He says "Afro-American" the same way my daddy used to say "nigger."

"Well?" he says when I don't answer right away. "Did you have to go all the way to New Orleans to get yourself some ghetto pussy?" He shakes his head. "That's pretty sad, man."

What I want to do more than anything right now is push his face down into the charcoal that's still burning in the bottom of the grill. Out of the corner of my eye I see Tiny, and he's watching both of us. The girls don't get it yet, they just walked up, but Peyton and Archie can tell that this could get bad real quick. The thing is, I can't tell whose side they're going to be on.

I'm all mixed up right now. I know what Daddy would do and what he would expect me to do. If I don't do some real damage to this asshole, I can just hear Daddy saying, "I knew you wouldn't amount to anything. Now if you were more like your brother, blah, blah, blah . . . . " The way he saw things, if I don't fight right now, I'm not worth a damn.

Mark's in my head, too, though, going on about what a good person I am. And so is Charlotte, telling me that Raymond must have seen something in me that reminded him of himself.

Then Gamaliel shows up, and he just looks at me and says, "Boone, is this little prick really worth it? If I were you I wouldn't waste my time."

They're all in my head, all talking at the same time, and I can't sit still anymore, so I stand up. Neil's sitting across from me and Tiny's off to my right. Nobody moves or says anything. Then Tiny leans forward a little, and everybody looks at him.

Chapter Twenty-Two

"Neil, I can tell you right now you don't want to take Boone on," Tiny says.

I'm standing here in front of everybody, and I don't know what to do next, and I don't know the best way out of this. That was the thing about Daddy. He always knew what to do. Usually it was the wrong thing, but he never worried about it. He just went right on. Sometimes he took a real beating, but he never changed. It might have been a stupid way to live, but that was how he did it.

I know a lot of people who feel the same way Neil does about black people. Hell, for all I know Peyton and Archie agree with him, and Jill and Miranda might, too. I don't know for sure about Tiny, but I don't think he'd say anything to me even if he thought I was in the wrong to do it with a black girl.

I mean, I was raised to feel that way, too. Most of us were, as far as I know. It wasn't until I got to know Mark that I had any dealings with black people at all.

I look around the circle, at Peyton and Archie and Neil, at Jill and Miranda still standing where they were when this all started, and at Tiny. He's trying to figure out what to do, too, I'll bet. It's his house and his party.

Neil's just sitting there with that stupid grin on his face, and I think about how he's acted the whole time I've been here, and then I think about Mark, and Louis and his brothers, and Mrs. Armstrong, and about Billie. Mostly I think about Mark and Billie. Then it comes to me, clear as air, what I need to do.

"Tiny," I say, "up until about a minute ago this was a real nice party, but I think me and Frankie are going to have to go. I'll holler at you tomorrow or the next day, maybe finish that story I was telling."

I look around at the rest of them. "It was real nice to meet y'all. Most of you, anyway." I walk over to Neil and I can see him tense up. He tries to keep grinning, but it's not working real well. I bend down so he's the only one that can hear me.

"You know," I say real soft, "if I gave a rat's ass about what you think I'd have to shove your face into those hot coals over there," I see him look at the grill, "but I don't. I might just be poor white trash and not much good with women, but at least I'm not you, and I'm real glad about that.

"I'm going to get out of here now before I change

258

my mind. Hope I never see you again, you worthless piece of shit."

I straighten up and look around again. "Thanks for the burger, Tiny. Y'all have a good day, now." My truck is at the end of the line, so I don't have to ask anybody to move. I see Frankie lying under a tree next to Eunuch and swing by to get her, and we walk to the truck.

Mark would have handled it better, I know that, but he's had a lot more practice than I have. Plus most of the time I bet he was all by himself with a bunch of people to stand against, and I just had a few that I wasn't sure about. I might have been on my own today, but I might not have been. I figure Mark was definitely on his own, over and over. That might be part of what he meant that time at the diner when I told him that I knew what it was like to be treated the way the waitress treated him, and he told me I didn't know what I was talking about.

Mark would have handled it without going over to Neil and calling him a worthless piece of shit, but I couldn't just let it go. Billie would probably have laughed at him and then ignored him completely, or said something to put him in his place. Miles, now, Miles would have done something, I'll bet. Of course none of them would have ever been at that party, so it doesn't really matter.

"Well, Frankie, where are we going to park this

thing tonight?" I reach over and scratch her ear and think about what would have happened if she had been beside me instead of up there with Eunuch when Neil started running his mouth. I'm kind of surprised she didn't feel how tense it was, but I guess she and Eunuch were talking about rabbits or skunks or something.

I might have had to put her on a leash to keep her off Neil. It would have been kind of fun to see him facing me and Frankie together, but I'll never know how that would have gone.

There's a place on the highway that has great ice cream and a drive through window, so I head that way. I still don't know where I'll sleep tonight, and that plus what happened just now at Tiny's party has me wondering. When I was out in Memphis it seemed like a real good idea to head back home, but now that I'm here it doesn't feel like home at all. The person living at the home that I like the most, Melvin, is about to die soon, Nancy doesn't want to have anything to do with me, and I got no home to go to. Hell, I don't even have a place to park the truck. Every place I stopped on this little trip felt better than the way this place is feeling right now.

I keep thinking I ought to talk to Mark. I know it's because he's black, or at least that's part of it, but when I think about my trip I got treated better in New Orleans than anywhere else. I mean, P. J. and

Joaquin treated me great, but the Armstrong family, that was different. Some of it was Billie, I know, but not all of it. They welcomed me right in and treated me better than anybody here has in I don't know when, maybe ever. Even after I really stepped in it with that thing I said about Mark, the only one who really got bent out of shape was Miles. It's weird that Daddy was so down on blacks and Mexicans and about everybody else, and I got treated better by a bunch of black people than I ever have by the people I grew up around. I really need to talk to Mark. Maybe he can help me figure this out.

There's a line at the drive through, but it's only about four or five cars long, and it moves pretty quick. I get a double scoop dipped in chocolate for me and a cup of vanilla for Frankie and we find a spot about halfway down the line of parked cars. I back in so I can drop the tailgate and sit there with Frankie without everybody staring at us while they drive by. Some people come here every other night and drive around and around, just killing time. I've already seen a couple of cars I recognize, and I don't care anything about talking to those guys I went to school with three or four years ago. I sit there and eat my ice cream, wondering why I even bothered coming back here.

I am glad I got to see Melvin again. I didn't know he was dying when I decided to head on back, but I'm glad I did it just so I could tell him about the trip. One thing surprised me, though; some of the stuff he was asking me about the night I spent with Billie was real personal, and once or twice I got pretty embarrassed. He had a great time with that, and thought it was hilarious that I didn't know what I was doing.

The rest of the stuff he knew about already. He even knew about Interstate Barbecue, and told me I had lucked into the best place in Memphis. I could tell right away that mostly what he was interested in was the people I met and the food I tried; he already knew about the beach, and the swamp, and Bourbon Street, and how flat Mississippi was, and even those guys on Beale Street doing flips for the tourists.

So that was a reason to come back, letting him know that his map was a good one. I'm going to hang on to it, since I only got to about half the places he circled. Should have told him that when I was in his room earlier, that I was going to keep traveling. He would have liked to hear that.

And it was real good to see Tiny, at least until Neil started his shit and pretty much ruined the evening for me. I wonder how it went after I left. I'll give Tiny a call in the next day or two and go by there again. He's a good guy and never looked down on me like most everybody here. Plus he had my back a couple of times when I really needed it.

I guess Melvin, and Tiny, and Mark are about the only good reasons to come back here that I'm seeing. There's no family here for me. Maybe the next trip I'll take will be up toward where Hannah is living now. I don't care much about seeing Aunt Claire, but me and Hannah always got along. She's really the only family I've got, since Momma is who knows where now, probably still with Jake.

I finish the cone. Frankie was finished with her cup a while ago and is starting to get a little restless, so I get her in the truck and go around to my door.

"Hey, Boone! Boone Hammond! Is that you?"

I look around and there's a girl hanging out of the window of a car that's driving by. She doesn't look like anybody I know. I wave at her and start to get in. She says something to whoever's driving and they stop right in front of the truck.

"Oh my God, I can't believe it! We were just talking about you!" She's out of the car now and standing on the other side of my truck door. She looks inside the truck. "Nancy isn't with you?"

I shake my head.

"Oh my God!" she says again. "You don't even know!"

I don't feel like talking to whoever this is about Nancy or anything else really. She's got me blocked, though, so it's not like I have a choice.

"Nancy and me, well, I haven't seen her for a

while," I say, "so I don't have a clue what you're talking about."

"It was awful, I mean, I wasn't there, but I heard it was awful. I mean, there wouldn't be any reason for me to be there, you know?"

I don't know how to talk to people that talk like this, so I don't say anything.

"Her brother was there, though, and he told us about it, that's how I know how bad it was!"

I start to say something but don't even get to say the first word.

"She and her dad had this huge fight! I mean, a monster fight, and she slammed her door and screamed through it that she never wanted to see him again. That's what Cyrus said, and he was there. He said he was just trying to stay out of his dad's way."

Sounds like old Stan put his foot down a little too hard and it blew up on him. Serves him right. She's still talking, and the next thing she says is nobody's seen Nancy since that night.

"That's why we were talking about you. You know I said we were just talking about you? Well, that's why. We figured she was with you. Cyrus says that's what her dad thinks, too, and he's about as mad at you as he's ever been at anybody. That's what Cyrus says. He says he wouldn't want to be you if her dad finds you."

Great. Why did I ever want to come back here? I know I'm sure as hell running out of reasons to stick around.

"I don't know what to tell you," I say. "She's not with me. I've been out of town for a couple of weeks, just me and Frankie."

"Who's Frankie?" she says. I point to Frankie, who's sitting in the passenger seat. "Oh!" she says. "Frankie's a dog!"

She stops talking then, like she's run out of stuff to say, and I don't really have anything to say to her. We just stand there for a minute and then she says, "Well, I better go."

"Me, too," I say. That's what I've been wanting to do since she blocked me in, but I don't say that.

She stands there like she's forgot which car she was in, and finally just turns around, walks back to her car, and gets in.

At first I'm really pissed off that she blocked me in, but after I get over that I'm glad. Better to know about Stan than to be surprised, in case he does come after me.

Nancy didn't tell me everything about her dad, but enough for me to know that her getting out is a good thing. I wonder who she ran away with; if that girl, whoever she is, says that everybody thinks she's with me, that means she didn't leave by herself. Probably she took off with some other guy.

A big part of me wishes it was me she left with. I started my trip wondering if she would have gone with me if I'd asked her to. It sounds like all I would have had to do is ask.

I'll bet that's why she got so mad when Tiny told her I was gone. She was probably pissed because I didn't ask her to go with me. There's no way I could have, with Stan and her mom on her all the time, but she kind of forgot about that, I guess.

We end up spending the night behind an old gas station that closed down four or five years ago and still has cars and trucks parked beside and behind it. We blend right in.

As soon as we get up I drive back to the home. I want to catch Mark early so I can get some time with him today. I know he usually has some stuff he can't get out of and the rest of his day starts out being open and fills up pretty fast. He's already in his office when we get there but tells me he's got some time right after lunch.

"What's this about, Boone?"

I don't know how to explain it, but he seems to be satisfied when I say that to him. We head back out with some time to kill before I can sit down with Mark.

Chapter Twenty-Three

"Let's see if Tiny's doing anything," I tell Frankie. "I'd like to know how the rest of the night went, anyway."

"Come on by," he says when I call him. "I'm just about ready to start on the oil changes, so I'll be here all morning."

I know Tiny's got his truck and an old car he's working on, plus his motorcycle, his mom's car, the farm truck, the four-wheelers, and a couple of tractors. I don't think he does the tractors very often, but even without them there's at least a half dozen oil changes, and Tiny never just does that. He's got to check the brakes and all the fluids, and he always finds something he didn't expect. I'll be surprised if he gets it all done by lunch.

When we get there he's underneath the old car he's been working on for at least the past year. I don't know where he picked it up or what he's going to do with it when he gets done. It's a Ford Ranchero, looks like somebody took a car and tried to make a truck out of the back half. I'm not sure what good it would be for hauling, but Tiny's always got something he's working on. This is his latest thing.

"Hey, Boone, hand me that rag," he says when he hears us come up.

"How'd you know it was me?"

"Your truck doesn't sound like any of ours."

I look around and find a rag, squat down and hand it to him.

"Man, I don't know what you said to Neil, but it fucked him up big time."

"No shit?" I can't say I'm sorry about that.

"No shit. I bet he didn't say ten words the rest of the night. I got to say it was kind of nice."

"He was a real asshole. How come you invited him?"

Tiny's quiet for a minute; I can barely hear him saying, "Come on, you stupid plug! Let loose!" Then he says, "Gotcha!" and slides out from under the car. "Gotta let that drain for a few minutes."

He cleans his hands up and says, "You want an S&S? It's a little early for me, but I'll fix you one if you want me to." He grabs a glass of water and takes a long drink.

I shake my head. "I'm good."

"Well," he says, "Neil doesn't really have any friends, so every once in a while I call him and tell him to come on by. What'd you say to him, anyway?"

"Nothing," I say. I'm feeling kind of bad right now about Neil. It's not like I had any friends either until Tiny and Nancy came along.

I guess I always figured if I had my brother Frankie I didn't need anybody else, so I didn't care all that much that the other kids treated us like shit. When he died, all of a sudden there wasn't anybody but Hannah, and she was just a little kid. I don't feel bad enough to go find Neil and tell him I'm sorry or anything, but still. I kind of wish I hadn't said what I did.

"He didn't need to say that stuff about Billie," I say.

"Yeah, about that," says Tiny. "You know it's a little weird, you going outside your own kind like that. I mean," he can see the look on my face, "I might have done the same thing, but we ought to stick together, you know? There's plenty of white girls around."

I guess I kind of half expected it, but it still is a hard thing to hear from him.

"I got to tell you, man, I didn't see anything wrong with it," I say. "Still don't."

"I get that," Tiny says. "I do. I just wouldn't go around bragging about it, is all."

I don't say anything. Nothing to say, really.

"What I want to hear about is that boat ride out

on the Mississippi," Tiny says. He really doesn't want to talk about this, which is okay. I don't either. "I've been out on the water all my life, but just on the lakes around here."

So I tell him about the boat ride that P. J. and Joaquin took us on. He's real interested in the barge, says that he would love to know what kind of motor it had in it. Then he looks away for a second and when he looks back he says, "Joaquin. That's a Mexican name, right?"

I shrug.

"So, was he a Mexican?"

I don't know whether he was or not. I never asked. He looked like a regular guy, and that's what I tell Tiny. He nods.

"A lot of them are okay. I just hate to see them coming up here and stealing jobs away from the local folks that have lived here their whole life."

"If you could have seen the boat, Tiny, I bet you would be knocked right on your ass. There's no way Joaquin's out picking tomatoes or anything else. I bet they've got as much money as y'all do."

He looks at me. "I said a lot of them are okay."

Right now it doesn't feel easy with Tiny like it used to. It's probably a bad idea to talk about my trip at all, and that's a shame because it was a great two weeks. I try to think of something else for us to talk about.

"I was at the drive through last night and some girl told me that Nancy had run off."

Tiny nods. "Yeah, just a couple of days ago."

"You knew about that already?"

He nods again. "If you hadn't taken off I was going to tell you after everybody was gone. I didn't think you'd want to talk about that in front of a bunch of people you didn't know."

"So what were you going to tell me? Where did she go? She leave with somebody?"

He takes his time answering. "Well, I don't know where she went. I mean, not for sure."

I'm getting a real bad feeling here.

"What does that mean, not for sure?"

"Well, she didn't say."

"She didn't say? How do you know that? Who'd she take off with?"

Tiny won't look at me. Then he takes a big breath and says, "I know that because when I dropped her off at the bus station in Knoxville she didn't say where she was going."

"You dropped her off?"

He nods. Now he's looking me right in the eye. "You know that note you left her? When I gave it to her and she was so pissed off that you were gone, I think it was because she was already planning to take off and she was going to call you. I took her because she didn't have anybody else she could trust.

271

You were gone, man. Otherwise, it would have been you she called."

"You dropped her off? Just like that?"

He nods.

I jump him but I think he must have been expecting it. He grabs my shoulders, spins me around, and wraps me up. I'm fighting as hard as I can, but he might as well be made out of concrete. Frankie is up and kind of growling, but she doesn't know what to do because it's Tiny. He sees that I'm looking at her and whispers, "Don't, man. Don't do it."

I'm still fighting, even though it's not getting me anywhere. I don't answer him.

"Come on, Boone. It's me. Tell Frankie you're okay. Don't make this into something real bad. Call her off."

I can't beat him, I know that. He's way too strong and he's got me so I can't get any kind of a hold. I ease up a little and say, "It's okay, Frankie. It's okay."

She doesn't move. There's still that low growl.

"She needs to see that I'm okay," I tell Tiny. "You got to ease up a little before she will."

He lets go real slow, and I get my feet under me solid and rub my arms where he had me wrapped up. "Come on, Frankie." I head toward the truck and she's right beside me.

"Hey, Boone," Tiny says, but I don't stop or even turn around. We get to the truck and get in, and I back up real slow and turn the truck around. I glance in the mirror while we're pulling away and he's standing there staring at me.

Chapter Twenty-Four

I spend a couple of hours driving around and finally go to the same drive through I was at last night and get a couple of burgers and some fries. We eat at one of their tables, under some trees off to the side. I'm still trying to figure out why Tiny would do that to me.

The more I think about it the madder I get, so I add it to the stuff I need to talk to Mark about. The way things are going I'll need all afternoon.

Mark is in his office sitting behind his desk when I get there. He tells me to come on in and I close the door behind us and sit down where I usually do. Frankie goes to her usual spot and lies down.

"Well," says Mark, "I would say this is like old times but you look like you've taken a real beating. Why don't you tell me what's eating you up inside and we'll see what we can do about it, you and I."

"I never got to tell you about my trip," I say, "and some stuff happened that I can't figure out. Plus some stuff since I got back, too, I guess."

He raises an eyebrow. "You just got back yesterday."

I nod. "Let me just tell it all to you. It's got me all screwed up inside, and I figure since you're a preacher I can tell you stuff, right?"

He nods. "It won't leave this room, Boone, if that's what you're worried about. It's not like you killed anybody or anything like that." He smiles a little but stops when he sees that I'm not.

"Okay, sorry, bad joke. Go ahead, Boone."

I start from just after I waved goodbye to him at the beginning of the trip and tell him everything that happened. He doesn't say a word or even react at all until I get to the part about Billie. Then he does the eyebrow thing again and says, "I see," and that's it. I wait for him to say something else and he doesn't, so I keep going.

When I tell him about Neil and all that stuff that happened last night at Tiny's he jerks a little, like somebody slapped him. I finish up with what happened this morning at Tiny's house, and once I stop talking he sits real still for what seems like a long time.

He's quiet for so long that I'm about ready to start talking again, but when I lean forward he holds up his hand. "I was just collecting my thoughts. You certainly have given me a lot to think about, Boone.

I'd like to say a few things to start off.

"You covered a lot of ground in the last couple of weeks, and while I don't personally agree with everything you did," he gives me a little smile, "I can understand the temptation."

"They treated me better than anybody ever has before," I say, "and I'm not just talking about Billie. Even Miles was okay until I said that stuff about you."

This time he laughs out loud. "I remember. So it doesn't even bother you that I'm black, Boone?"

I grin at him. Then I look down at the floor.

"The thing is, Mark, before I met you and the Armstrongs, that shit Neil was saying last night probably wouldn't have bothered me near as much. I'm not proud of that, but it's the truth."

We're both quiet for a minute after I say that.

"That's one thing about you that I appreciate, Boone," he says. "I can trust that you're going to tell me the truth. Not everyone who sits in that chair does, you know."

I think back to all the times I've sat here, and I'm sure that I've lied to him at least a few times. Maybe not as much now as I used to, though.

"What am I supposed to do about Tiny and Nancy?"

Mark looks a little confused. "What do you mean?"

"You know," I say.

277

He shakes his head. "I don't see that Tiny did anything wrong, Boone. He didn't take off with your girl. He just gave her a ride. I might fault him for getting in the middle of a family dispute, but the way I see it, it's less than what you would have done if you'd been here."

I stare at him. "You're taking his side?"

"There's no side here for me to take, Boone. If you're worried about there being something going on between Tiny and Nancy, there's nothing here to suggest that."

Sometimes it just pisses me off that he can be so right about stuff. I know he's right, there's nothing going on between them, and I know I shouldn't have jumped Tiny like I did, but now that it's done I don't know what to do.

"Do you want me to talk to Tiny for you?" Mark asks.

I shake my head.

"Good," he says. "I don't know that I could do that. Like I said, there's no side for me to take, and I think you and Tiny can work this out. You might give him a day or two."

I nod. "I know, I know. It just hit me wrong, I'm not sure why."

Mark laughs. "Give it a little thought."

I look at him and then away from him. "I don't know what the hell you're talking about, man. She doesn't want to see me ever again, she told Tiny that, and it's fine with me. She can go wherever she wants to."

We sit there quiet for a minute. Mark says, "It's okay to feel bad about losing her, Boone. You two were really good together."

If we keep on talking about her I'm going to start crying like a little kid.

"Well, what about me and Billie?"

Mark takes a second to answer. "There is no you and Billie, Boone, I think you know that."

"I know that, man. There's no way I could find her again if I went back down there, and I don't think she'd even want me to try. I mean, what do you think about what happened? Come on, Mark, I'm pretty mixed up here, and there's not a lot of people I can talk to about this."

He takes his time answering me.

"I think there are a few questions here. Are you asking me because I'm a black man, or because I'm a preacher, or for some other reason?"

"It's like you said about me a minute ago. You'll tell me the truth. I don't know a lot of people that do that."

He nods. "Thank you for that, Boone."

Then he just sits there.

Finally I say, "Well? Are you going to tell me something here?"

Mark clears his throat. "I've been working here for a while now, worked with people of all different faiths and some with no faith at all, and one thing I've learned is that it is not my place to pass judgment. I can meet people where they are. That seems to work best for everyone.

"I can't speak for black people as a race, either. If you are looking for somebody who can tell you how all black people feel about interracial, um, relations, I'm afraid you won't get that from me."

This is pretty damn frustrating.

"So you're not going to help me out here?"

"Oh, I didn't say that. I can listen to you and tell you what I think you're saying, and you'll know if I'm getting it right."

"Okay, I'll tell you what I think. I think I'm damn lucky that somebody as smart and pretty as Billie even noticed that I was alive, much less took me home with her, and it doesn't bother me a bit that she's black."

He smiles at me. "So where's the problem?"

"Damn, Mark, I just about put Neil's face in the hot coals last night, and today I tried to take on Tiny even though I knew how stupid that was. Poor Frankie didn't know what to do, me going up against him. That's a problem right there."

"Sounds like you almost started a couple of fights since you got back, but ended up walking away from both of them."

"Well, yeah, but . . . "

I have to stop for a second.

"Okay, I don't give a damn about Neil one way or the other, but Tiny's maybe the best friend I've got in the world."

He just sits there.

"Aren't you going to say something?"

He shakes his head. "You're doing fine all by yourself. I'd just get in the way."

I stand up, but there's not really enough room in this place to walk around much, so I end up sitting back down.

"It pisses me off that all these people around here think they're better than me and anybody I hang out with. I mean, who the hell do they think they are, anyway?"

I lean back in the chair and cross my arms. I'm not getting any less mad, seems like. Frankie is still right where she laid down when we came in. I look over at her and then down at the floor, talking mostly to myself.

"I mean, why am I wasting my time with those assholes, anyway?"

"That's an important question. A little crudely put, but definitely an important question."

When I look up at Mark, he's nodding at me.

"You owe Melvin more than you know, Boone. I

281

think this trip is another big step for you, and it all started when you became friends with him."

This isn't helping me at all. Mark's talking about all this stuff and all I want to do is just stop being so pissed off. I went on this trip and met all kinds of really decent people. Well, actually, Frankie met most of them and I just went along for the ride. Anyway, it was a good two weeks, and then I come back here and it's the same old shit.

Maybe we just need to get back in the truck and head on out again. There's places on Melvin's map we didn't get to, and I didn't really spend anything on this trip because of what Charlotte did.

I stand up again and say, "Listen, Mark, I got to get out of here and think about some stuff."

"I thought you might," he says. "The things you are starting to see are going to make your life more complicated. That is not a bad thing; it's actually very good. Right now I can tell you that Tiny is a good friend of yours, and it will be worthwhile to make things right with him."

I nod. "Yeah, I know."

Mark smiles a big smile. "Stop by anytime, Boone. I'd love to hear how you're doing figuring all this out."

Chapter Twenty-Five

I keep thinking about what P. J. said about me and animals. Maybe she's right. That's something I could be pretty good at, I guess, but I'm not for sure. The only animal I've been around a lot is Frankie. We get along great, a lot better than I get along with most people, but she's just one dog.

"You're the best dog, though, aren't you?" She's sitting next to me in the truck, and we're looking out over one of the Thompson fields. I can see one of their trucks over at the edge, and the big guy sitting on the tailgate has to be Tiny.

It's been a few days since I was up at his house and tried to take him on. It was so easy for him to stop me it was embarrassing, but I kind of knew it would go that way. I didn't think, though, I just went for it. That's something else Daddy taught me. Don't think about it, just go. That almost never worked out for him, and it didn't work out for me up at Tiny's either.

"All right, girl, this isn't going to get any easier if I wait til tomorrow," I say. "Let's go."

When I shut the door Tiny looks over towards me. I can see Eunuch out in the field and Frankie takes off toward him. Tiny slides off the tailgate when I'm about twenty feet away.

He doesn't come up to me. He's in the shade and I'm not, so that makes sense. I walk up to him and say, "Hey, Tiny."

"Boone, how's it going?"

I hadn't really thought about what I was going to say, so we both just stand there for a minute. Finally I say the only thing I can think of, which is "How's Eunuch?" and I know as soon as I say it how stupid that sounds.

"He's fine."

I'm about ready to turn around and head back to the truck, but I decide what the hell, I'm here and I might as well say something more than how's your dog.

"Listen, man, about the other day . . . "

He stands there, doesn't say a damn word. We look at each other for a minute and then he smiles just a little bit. Then he starts laughing and says, "Man, you are hating this, aren't you?"

I can feel my face getting red and I'm starting to get mad all over again, but then for some reason it hits me as funny, too, and I start laughing right along with him.

After I catch my breath I say, "Man, you stood there and let me do that, didn't you?"

He shrugs. "Damn right I did."

He's still grinning, but I know now that I've started I need to finish it up.

"Listen, Tiny, I was out of line. It hit me wrong and I didn't even think, you know?"

He doesn't say anything for a second, and then he nods. "I wondered if you'd have the balls to come back and face me after that."

"Wasn't going to, but then I thought, I've tried stupid and that didn't work." I shrug. "So, are we okay?"

"Always were," he says. "Just don't jump me again, all right?"

"Like I said, I've tried stupid already." I look at him. "You didn't have to squeeze that hard, you know."

He shakes his head. "I know you, Boone. You're a sneaky son of a bitch. I figured if I didn't hold on pretty tight I'd be in trouble before I knew it."

"Damn right," I say, grinning.

He doesn't ask me any more about Billie, and I don't volunteer anything. He tells me some more about Nancy, though. She must have talked to him a little bit while he was giving her a ride. Sounds like Stan got to be such an asshole about keeping her in sight all the time that she figured the only thing she could do was run.

"I hate that for her," Tiny says. "She's a real nice girl, doesn't have a mean bone in her body, and he's treating her like shit. Now it's gone and blown up in his face. Who knows where she'll end up?"

Only thing I can do is nod. Then I think to ask, "Did she have any money?"

Tiny shrugs. "I guess so. I mean, she didn't ask for any."

I'm feeling guilty as hell right now for taking off on my own little trip while she was hurting so much.

"It's not your fault," Tiny says.

"What?"

"Nancy said that, just before I dropped her off. She said if her dad thought she was with you he might shoot you the next time he saw you, or at least beat you up. Said she told her mother about your trip a day or so before she took off, how you were gone and she didn't know where, or even how to get hold of you. She probably saved your ass from a real beating, because Stan was looking for you. He asked me if you were in town, and I told him the same thing Nancy told her mother. I'm pretty sure he believed me. If I were you, though, I'd still go the other way if I ever saw him coming."

"I believe I'll do that," I say. "Truth is, I'm not sure how long I'll be around here for him to find."

"Man, you just got back. You're leaving again?"

"I don't know yet."

That's the truth, but I think I'm starting to get close to making up my mind.

Tiny and I talk about this and that for the next hour or two. We watch the dogs chase each other around the field and finally fall asleep in the shade next to the fence row. I got to say it's good to have things set right with Tiny. I'll just have to remember not to talk to him about black people or Mexicans. I don't like that much, but Tiny's about the only friend I've got around here with Nancy gone.

When I mention to Tiny what P. J. said about me and animals, he nods his head. "I hadn't thought about it before, but I think she's right. You do have kind of a way with them, at least from what I've seen."

I don't think I've been around that many, but if Tiny's seen it too maybe there's something to that.

After a minute or two he says, "If you're thinking about one of the animal shelters around here, you ought to know that they kill a lot of dogs and cats in those places."

"What the hell are you talking about?"

I had this picture of a place that saved all these animals like Frankie that were going to be tossed in the river or something, and found places for them. I say that to Tiny and he nods. "Right. That is what they do. But they can't find homes for all of them, right? Some of them are old, or crippled, or mean, or just ugly, and nobody wants them. So they have to kill them."

Well, if that's part of the deal at those places, there's no way in hell I'd work there. Ever since Memphis I'd been kind of halfway thinking about trying to do that kind of thing, but that's not going to happen now. No way.

So what am I going to do now? I could get back on the road and go until I spent all of Gamaliel's money, but then I'd have the same problem that I've got right now, except I'd be broke.

Raymond said he thought I would find some kind of useful work, but I think he might be full of shit about that. I don't really know how to do much of anything. I'm not like him, some kind of computer genius or something. Hell, I don't even have a high school diploma.

I can't think about this kind of stuff for very long without starting to really feel like shit, so I try to think about something else. I'm not coming up with anything, and then Tiny says, "Are you for real thinking about going right back out?"

Okay. I'd rather talk about that anyway.

"Well, there's a lot of places on Melvin's map I didn't get to, and he only did a little bit of the country, so, yeah, I'm thinking about it. He told me when we were first talking about it that I ought to go while I was young and didn't have a job or anything like that to keep me here."

"Man, there's gotta be something here." Tiny looks real uncomfortable, and I'm not sure why.

"Not really. I mean, look. I've got you, and Mark, and Melvin. Melvin's about to die any day now. And that's it. I got no family here, no job, no place to live. I really don't have a great big reason to stay."

"Well," he says, "when you say it like that." He looks over at me. "You couldn't get your job back at the home?"

"Hell, Tiny, that wasn't a job. That was charity. I didn't do hardly anything there and they fed me, gave me a place to stay, a little money for, you know, whatever. It got to where I couldn't take it anymore. I mean, even if Melvin hadn't pushed me I would have been out of there before too long."

Even while I'm saying that I know it's not true. If it hadn't been for him I'd still be sitting on my ass doing just about nothing and getting paid for it.

"So when are you taking off?"

I shrug. "I don't even know where I'm going, so I don't really know."

"You need a place to stay? We've got room at the house, and Mom would love to have you around. God knows why, but she likes you." He grins.

"I appreciate it, but I've gotten kind of used to

coming and going whenever I feel like it. Staying in somebody else's house would just be too weird."

Tiny hollers for Eunuch. "Listen, I got to get out of here. Next time you decide to jump me like the other day, bring a couple of guys with you. I might not go easy on you next time."

"Hell, I wasn't half trying the other night. You ought to start lifting weights or something, you know, just in case."

"I already am." He slams the tailgate, reaches down and grabs the trailer hitch, and picks up the rear end of the truck. He holds it for a count of ten and then drops it. It bounces a couple of times. "Got my weight set right here with me."

Even though I can see that the bed's empty and I know almost all the weight in a pickup is in the front, it's still pretty damn impressive. I don't let on, of course.

"Not bad. Could have been a little higher, but I can tell you were really trying hard."

He laughs that short laugh. "You better get your ass on down the road, Boone. You're about an inch away from some real trouble."

"Right," I say. "There's a couple more places I got to stop by this afternoon, so I can't stick around anyway. Come on, Frankie!"

We start back to the truck and get about halfway there when Tiny hollers at us.

"Hey, Boone!"

I turn around. He's got Eunuch in the cab already and is about to get behind the wheel.

"Don't take off without stopping by."

Chapter Twenty-Six

We spend the rest of the afternoon driving around, not going anywhere in particular. We need a chance to talk. After about an hour we end up at a little picnic area on the side of the road. I guess the state must have built it a while back. It has one of those concrete picnic tables and a grill on a post that looks like nobody's used it or cleaned it in about a dozen years. There's a creek on the back side and a place to sit next to the water.

"So, Frankie, what do you think we ought to do? Hit the road again or stick around here for a while?"

She's got her head down on her front paws, and she's staring at the water.

"Here's what I'm thinking," I say. "If we stay here I've got to find a place to live and I guess I ought to get some kind of job. Don't really know how to do either one of those things, so I'd have to figure that out.

"If we take off now, I'll have to use some more of

that money that Gamaliel left. There's no way we're going to come out ahead the way we did on this last one. That was all about what happened with Raymond and Charlotte, and that's not going to happen again."

I stop and wait for Frankie to say something, but she's still just watching the water.

"If we stay, I know that there's some stuff that's going to be pretty hard for me to deal with. The stuff that happened with that waitress and with Neil, I know there's a lot of people around here feel that same way. Hell, until just the last little while I didn't have any real problem with it either. But I do now, and I know if I stay here I'm going to run into that shit over and over. I figure it's got to be better somewhere else.

"The thought of moving somewhere else scares the hell out of me, to be honest with you. I wouldn't tell just anybody that, but it's the damn truth. The thing is, the people who live here that knew my daddy are going to figure me to be just like him. That's not a lot of people, but enough, I think, to make it hard to stick around. And if I moved away from here, nobody would know about what an asshole my daddy was, so I wouldn't have to try to live that down. I've been trying ever since he died to get rid of all that shit he taught me, and I think that'd be easier if I were somewhere else."

Frankie looks over at me and I swear it looks like she's saying, "So how are you doing at getting rid of all that shit your daddy taught you?"

"I know, I know. Every time I get my back against the wall the first thing I want to do is the exact thing he would do. Even if I know it's the worst way I could go.

"But I'm trying, girl, I really am."

She's back to watching the water go by. I'm just going around and around here, so I give up and join her. We end up spending the night there. There's not a whole lot of traffic, and nobody else pulls in to use the place.

The next morning I drive through a place out on the highway that does breakfast and get some bacon biscuits and coffee. It's not Benton's bacon, but it's not too bad. Then I head back over toward the home to try to catch Mark and see if he's got any time today. I can't sort all this out by myself, and he already knows most of what's going on.

The first person I run into is Betty.

"Boone, I was hoping you'd stop back by! Do you have a few minutes?"

I'd be lying if I said no, but that's what I really want to say.

"Sure, Betty. What's up?"

She grabs my arm. "Why don't we get out of the hallway?" She turns me toward the side hall where her office is. "Frankie, you want to join us?"

When we get to her office, she closes the door behind us and goes around to sit behind her desk.

"Well, how was your trip? Mark told me a little about it, but I'd love to hear what you thought. It sounds like you did a quick tour of the Southeast, and I think that would be just lovely."

I tell her a little bit about it, leaving out the guys in the parking lot at the swamp and my night with Billie. She seems real interested in what P. J. said about me and animals.

"If you want I can ask around," she says. "You and Frankie certainly did a lot of good work here, and I have a few people I could speak to."

"I'd appreciate that, Betty. I'm not sure about what I'm going to do next, but if you wouldn't mind," I say. "When I mentioned it to Tiny he said that those animal shelters end up having to kill a lot of the dogs and cats that end up there, and I'm pretty sure I couldn't do that."

She gets quiet for a second. "I know, Boone. It breaks my heart, thinking about all those poor creatures. I'm sure there must be somewhere you could work where you wouldn't have to be a part of that."

I nod. I'm about to ask if that's all she wanted to talk about when she clears her throat and says, "Of course, that's not why I wanted to talk to you."

It's been a long time since I've been called to a principal's office, but what she said and the way she said it feels just like I'm sitting in one.

She leans forward. "It's about Nancy. Her mom and I, well, we've known each other for years, and she told me about what happened. Now, she didn't ask me to talk to you, Boone. I'm doing this because she's a dear friend of mine. If Nancy is with you or if you know where she is, I'd like for you to call her," she pushes a piece of paper across to me, "at this number. It's her cell."

I don't pick it up.

Betty goes on, "I don't want to know anything about your involvement in this. I like you, Boone, I'm sure you know that. Whatever was going on between Nancy and her father was already ripping the family apart, and now this . . . ."

It looks like she's about to start bawling right there in front of me and Frankie.

Real quick, before she can either start talking again or crying, I say, "Betty, I didn't even know Nancy was gone until night before last. I was at a cookout at Tiny's and he told me. He doesn't know where she is, just that she's gone, and he knew it wasn't me because he knew when I left town."

I lean back in the chair. "Come to think about it, so did you. You knew I was already gone. What the hell is going on here, Betty?"

297

Betty spreads her hands. "When I said she didn't ask me to talk to you, I didn't say that I was doing it behind her back. She knows that we know each other. Last night she was on the phone with me, just crying her heart out, and I said I would ask. She's a friend of mine, Boone. I hope you can understand that."

I get it, but I sure as hell don't like it.

"I don't get why people think I was part of this whole thing," I say, loud enough that Frankie raises her head up. "When this happened, I was in Georgia, or Louisiana, or Memphis. I sure as hell wasn't here." I take a big breath and try to calm down.

"Look. I've met Nancy's mom, she seems like a nice lady. Makes a great pie. I'm real sorry she's hurting right now, but I didn't do anything and I don't know anything. I can't help her out, don't have any idea where Nancy might go, or who she might be with." That last part feels kind of bad since I know that Tiny took her to the bus station, but he doesn't really know anything either.

We sit there for what seems like a long time, sort of not looking at each other, until she sighs real loud. "Okay, Boone, I'll tell her. I had to try. You can't understand how a mother would feel, wondering where her child is or if they're okay."

I get so mad, so quick, that I know if I don't leave right now I'm going to say something I shouldn't. I stand up and say, "Come on, Frankie, we need to get out of here."

When we get to the door I turn and look at Betty. She looks confused, so I say, "You probably forgot that my momma left me a while back. I got no idea where she is or who she's with." I try not to slam the office door on my way out, but it still sounds really loud in the hallway. I think she says something when I'm halfway out the door, but I don't turn around to find out. Whatever it is, I don't want to hear it.

Mark is in the main hallway when I turn the corner heading for the front door. I don't even slow down, but he follows me out into the parking lot.

"Hey, Boone, wait up."

I'm about to open the truck door, but I stop and let him catch up.

"What's wrong?"

"Nothing."

"Something must be. You were practically running out of the building."

"Maybe you ought to ask Betty."

Mark shakes his head. "She told me she's been talking to Nancy's mother. Betty asked you where Nancy was, didn't she?"

I nod.

"So what did you say to her?"

I turn to face him. "She knew I was already gone, just like you did. She didn't have to ask me like that, like she thought I'd sneaked back into town and stole her or something. I'm tired of getting accused of shit I didn't do!"

I'm almost shouting, and I know it's not Mark I'm mad at, but it's still real hard to settle down. He doesn't say anything right away, lets me get myself back together. Then he says, "You know, she's more worried about her friend than anything else. I'm sure she didn't mean to come across like she was accusing you of anything."

I stare at him for a second, and then nod. "Yeah, I know. Still pisses me off."

"I can tell. As it happens, I was just heading out for a cup of coffee. There's a new cafe in town, and I've heard they have the best coffee and Danish in the county. Why don't you two come with me? We'll sit out on their patio. My treat."

Frankie and I stay outside while Mark goes in. He comes out with two huge coffees and two Danishes, which look like cinnamon rolls but they have some kind of stuff in the middle and they're twice the size. It's not been all that long since I had that bacon biscuit, but they look really good.

"The owners must be pet lovers," Mark says. He points to a water dish set off in the shade next to the building. I take Frankie over for a quick drink. When we get back I try the Danish. It's real good, and so is the coffee. Mark takes a sip of his and says, "Now that's a latte."

I don't know what a latte is, and I guess it shows.

"It's made with espresso and milk," Mark says. "You can get it with all kinds of flavors. I like the caramel, but there's a whole list in there on the wall. Want to try it?" He slides it over to me.

I take a sip and, I have to say, the coffee and caramel together is awfully good.

"I told you," Mark says with a grin. "Now, I've got some time if you want to talk."

My Danish is about half gone already. I take another bite and a long drink of coffee and start talking.

Mark doesn't interrupt except a couple of times, and I lay out pretty much everything that's on my mind, from how much different everybody seems since I got back, to whether I should stick around or not, about getting a job here or somewhere else, and how the way I feel now about black people seems like just one more thing for people to look down on me about. And there's Nancy. I don't know what to do about that. And since Betty brought it up, there's Momma and Hannah, and I don't know what to do about that either.

"Well," says Mark when I finally run out of stuff to say, "that's quite a list. You know there's no possible way for you to tackle all those at once, and besides, some of them aren't the kinds of things you have control over. It seems like a good first step

301

would be to separate all these things into the ones you can do something about and the ones that either may not change at all, or depend mostly or entirely on someone else.

"I think whether you go or stay is completely up to you, and so is deciding to look for a job. Most of the rest of it, you have to decide how much of it you can realistically expect to do anything about. The attitudes of the people around here—or anywhere else, for that matter—aren't yours to change, of course. Your mother, your sister, and Nancy, well, you only know where one of them even is, so that's a difficult problem to address."

"You're right, man, I mean, you usually are. But one thing that's really got me all mixed up is, you know, after you and the Armstrongs, mostly Billie, changed the way I feel about black people, I just look at all these people around here different."

"Let me ask you this, Boone. Do you feel the same way about Neil as you do about Tiny?"

"Hell, no, I can't believe you're even asking me that. Neil's an asshole, and Tiny, well, Tiny's the best friend I've got in the world."

"And yet they're both white. I'm very glad you've had a good experience with black people so far, but I have to caution you against making any kind of blanket judgment. Just as all white people aren't alike, neither are all black people, and I would encourage you not to lump us all together into one homogenous group."

I get what he's saying, but it's not making things any simpler for me.

He's still talking. "I've heard you describe yourself as poor white trash. I would agree with two of those things. You are most certainly not trash. I know that when you assign that label to yourself you put yourself into a group that you actually have very little in common with. It's a risky thing, lumping people together like that, even though it makes it easy to pass judgment."

I give him a look and he grins like he's a little embarrassed.

"Too preachy, right?"

"Yeah, a little bit. It's all right, though. You let me talk, so I figure I ought to let you talk."

He points to my cup. "You want a refill?"

"I don't know. Do they have that latte stuff in a small size?"

Chapter Twenty-Seven

I get a phone call from Mark about Melvin two days later.

"He's gone, Boone. It happened last night, very peaceful. The service is day after tomorrow, and I thought you might want to know."

"Thanks, Mark. At the chapel?"

"Yes, most of his friends are here at the home and a lot of them don't travel. It's set for 2:30."

"I appreciate you letting me know. Listen, Mark, can you tell me where to get some new clothes? My stuff's kind of ratty to wear to a funeral."

He laughs real soft, but I still hear it. "I do know a couple of places. Would you like me to go with you?"

I tell him yes, and that I'm not talking about a suit or anything, just some new jeans and maybe a decent shirt or two.

We meet the next day a little before lunch. He takes me to two different places and at one of them it's kind of hard to get anybody to wait on us. I'm about to tell them all to go to hell and walk out, but Mark lays a hand on my arm and says, "Give it a second."

When we finally get somebody she acts like she's better than either one of us, but I do get a pair of jeans and a shirt that looks halfway decent. "You need a belt," Mark says, and we get one of those, too.

He talks me into a haircut, and after that we get sandwiches and fries at a place he knows about but I've never eaten at. The sandwich isn't really any better than any other sandwich I've had, but it's okay, and Mark seems to like the place a lot.

"You clean up real good, Boone," he says.

I'm trying to remember the last time I bought new clothes that never had belonged to anybody else, and finally give up. Momma always went to those second hand stores because they were so cheap.

"There is one thing," he says. He looks down at my feet.

I almost walk out of the shoe store, too, but not because I'm getting treated bad. Shoes are damned expensive. Mark won't let it go, though, and I get a pair of what they call cross trainers, and some new socks while I'm there.

I've never had shoes this comfortable before. Not in my whole life.

We get back to our cars and Mark says, "I think Gamaliel would approve of you spending a small part of that money the way you did today. You look great. I'm wondering if Betty will even recognize you."

I hadn't even thought about Betty being there. He sees the look on my face and says, "Give her a chance, Boone. She was worried about her friend."

The bad thing about having new clothes, and new shoes especially, is that now I don't feel like I can just throw them in the back of the truck like I've done with all my other clothes before, and I'm looking at where I step so I won't get anything on my shoes. It's a lot of work.

They still look okay when I get to the chapel, I guess, and I get inside just before Mark starts talking. Betty is sitting way up front, so that's good. I don't have to say anything to her. I sit down close to the door and listen to Mark. He's pretty good at this stuff, especially if he kind of knows who he's talking about.

Then he says, "Boone, if you'd be willing to come up and say a few words, I know we'd all appreciate it. I know Melvin inspired your recent trip around the Southeast."

I give him a dirty look, but now everybody's looking at me and smiling, so I stand up and tell Frankie to stay where she is. When I step up next to Mark he leans over and whispers, "Thanks, Boone. I think Melvin would appreciate it, too."

It's a lot easier, and a lot shorter, than it was with

Gamaliel's service. Aside from the trip, there's not too much I can tell them. I leave out the parts about the guys in Georgia and my night with Billie, but they all seem to like hearing about the rest of it, and I get through it without crying the way I did at Gamaliel's. When I start back down Betty catches my eye and it looks like she says, "Thank you," but I can't hear it.

When it's over I try to get out of there as quick as I can so I don't have to talk to anybody, and it almost works. Betty catches me just outside the chapel door and takes my arm.

"Boone, I know what I said the other day was a mistake, and I'm sorry as I can be," she says. "I was so worried about Nancy that I didn't think about how you might feel about what I said. I'm sorry."

"It's okay, Betty, it just hit me wrong," I say, and it's true. It is okay. She didn't mean anything by it. I know that.

"I appreciate that. Now, I need to go be with his family for a bit. Thanks for coming, and for telling us about your trip."

She hurries off, and Frankie and I head for the truck. I get out of my good shirt and do a kind of half ass job of folding it up. I put on a tee shirt and feel a lot better.

There's not a lot of places to eat where you can just drive through, so we end up at the same place we've eaten twice before already. We don't eat in the parking lot this time. Instead we go back to the place by the side of the road and eat at the picnic table. I figure it's as good a place as any to spend the night.

The next morning I get out Melvin's map and spread it on the hood of the truck. Ever since the service he's been in my head, talking about all the neat places there are to see.

I kind of go over where I went this last time, and that makes me think about Abigail, and Raymond and Charlotte, and P. J. and Joaquin. I wouldn't have any idea how to track down either Jericho or the Armstrongs, but I'm looking at the map thinking, I could go see Abigail, she's just down the road. Raymond and Charlotte are up in Virginia, that's what Charlotte said in her note, in something called the Shenandoah Valley, and when I find that on the map it's not all that far away. And P. J. and Joaquin, I'm not sure exactly where they are in Memphis, but I've got P. J.'s cell number somewhere.

When I decide to make a list I realize that I don't have any paper, so I tear the bag the food came in down the side and open it out. I make a list of some of the places Melvin had circled that I didn't see the first time out, and another list of the people I met I'd like to see again. This is starting to sound pretty good.

"Hey, Frankie, what do you think about taking a few short trips instead of another long one?"

She's too busy taking a nap to answer me, so I end up talking to myself.

"I could start with going down to the Ocoee and trying to find Abigail." I'm talking out loud even though it's just to me. Then I remember I've got her phone number. "Okay. She'll be easy to find."

I'm looking in the glove compartment for her phone number and run across Raymond's card with his number on it, so I'm good to go for them, too, and I know P. J.'s is in here somewhere.

I write all the phone numbers on the list next to the names and sit back, looking at what I've got. It looks like I've decided what I'm going to do next. There's four or five places that Melvin said were really great. I might do one or two of those before I track down Raymond or P. J., but I'm thinking that since the Ocoee is just down the road I ought to go see Abigail pretty soon.

The next day I track down Tiny and let him know what I'm getting ready to do.

"I'm not surprised," he says. "You didn't talk like you were done traveling. Know where you're going?"

I show him the list and say, "That's probably more than one trip."

He laughs. "You think?"

I stick out my hand and we shake. "Take care of Eunuch," I say. "Frankie would be pretty pissed if you let anything happen to him while we're gone."

He nods. "Next time, S&Ss down at the lake. We'll take a couple of poles and pretend we're going fishing."

"You got it."

Later on I go see Mark to tell him what I'm doing. I run into Betty as soon as I walk in, and she starts apologizing again.

"It's okay, Betty, really," I say.

"You're sure?" she asks.

I nod, and she gives me a hug, which feels weird, since she doesn't do that kind of thing much. Then she says, "I have a meeting with the family of a new resident in ten minutes. If you're looking for Mark, he should be finishing with them about now."

He's not at his office when we get there, but he shows up about three minutes later.

"Come on in, Boone. Figured anything out yet?"

I know he's talking about all that serious stuff we talked about, so I shake my head. "No, not yet. I'll figure it out eventually, I guess. One thing I did decide is about staying here or taking another trip."

"Let me guess. You're back on the road."

I nod. "All during the service I was thinking about some of the stuff Melvin said, about doing this while I still can, before I get a job and all that stuff."

"Do you know where you're going first?"

When I tell him I'm going to see Abigail, he grins. "Going rafting?"

"Well, I don't know about that. We'll see." I'm grinning, too.

I show him the list and he looks it over.

While he's doing that I look around the office. I've spent a fair amount of time here, from the first time I met him when he did Gamaliel's service, all the way through the shit I went through with Jerry, the fire up at Tiny's, my problems with Nancy, Aunt Claire popping in out of nowhere to hassle me about Momma, and those talks about nothing in particular. He catches me staring at him and asks, "Something the matter?"

I shake my head.

He leans back in his chair. "You sure?"

I nod, and then, before I even think about what I'm saying, I say, "You know, you and Gamaliel and Melvin, but mostly you and Gamaliel, I mean . . . " I kind of trail off and he just sits there, waiting. I guess preachers learn how to do that. Wait.

"I just appreciate you. That's all."

He bows his head. "Thank you, Boone."

"Well, you know, after Daddy . . ." Right then I come closer to telling somebody what really happened with Daddy, and what I did about it, than I ever have before.

I don't do it, though. I mean, I like Mark, and I trust him as much as I do anybody, plus he's a preacher and I know he can keep a secret.

But I still don't do it. I think it's better if I'm the only one that knows what really happened. As far as I'm concerned, I didn't do anything wrong. My Daddy spent his whole life making one mess after another. All I did was clean up the last one.

End of Book Four

CPSIA information can be obtained
at www.ICGtesting.com
Printed in the USA
LVHW021035030621
689238LV00005B/453

9 781734 673852